NICOLA
BERRY

FOR ANNA
— L M

PENGUIN WORKSHOP
Penguin Young Readers Group
An Imprint of Penguin Random House LLC

Penguin supports copyright. Copyright fuels creativity, encourages
diverse voices, promotes free speech, and creates a vibrant culture.
Thank you for buying an authorized edition of this book and for
complying with copyright laws by not reproducing, scanning,
or distributing any part of it in any form without permission.
You are supporting writers and allowing Penguin to
continue to publish books for every reader.

Text copyright © 2010 by Liane Moriarty.
Cover illustration copyright © 2018 by Rebecca Mock.
All rights reserved. First published in 2010 as
Nicola Berry: Earthling Ambassador: War on Whimsy
by Grosset & Dunlap. This edition published in 2018 by
Penguin Workshop, an imprint of Penguin Random House LLC,
345 Hudson Street, New York, New York 10014.
PENGUIN and PENGUIN WORKSHOP are trademarks
of Penguin Books Ltd, and the W colophon is a trademark
of Penguin Random House LLC. Printed in the USA.

Cover illustration by Rebecca Mock
Design by Sara Corbett
The text in this book is set in Surveyor.

The Library of Congress has cataloged the Grosset & Dunlap
edition under the following Control Number: 2009024831

ISBN 9781524788100   10 9 8 7 6 5 4 3 2 1

LIANE MORIARTY

NICOLA BERRY

AND THE WICKED WAR ON THE PLANET OF WHIMSY

PENGUIN WORKSHOP ★ AN IMPRINT OF PENGUIN RANDOM HOUSE

PROLOGUE

N EXTREMELY TALL MAN AND WOMAN huddled together in a small, damp, dark cell.

Their nostrils were filled with the scent of roses. Their mouths were dry from thirst and fear.

A little boy lay asleep on the woman's lap, his thumb in his mouth.

"We should never have done it," whispered the woman. She brushed away a leftover teardrop from the little boy's face.

"Maybe not," sighed the man.

"What do you think she'll do?"

This time the man smiled, his teeth a sudden flash of white in the darkness.

"She'll call Nicola, of course."

I

NICOLA! PHONE CALL!"

Nicola Berry was startled. Who would be calling her here at this time of night?

"For me? Really?"

It was past midnight and she was at her great-grandmother's one-hundredth birthday party. The music was thumping, and Grammy was tapping her feet and jiggling her hips, leaning on a walking stick in each hand. Nicola and her cousins were all hiding yawns as they danced in a circle around their tiny, white-haired grandmother, who might have been the oldest one at the party, but seemed to have the most energy. The littler cousins were asleep, curled up in corners. Even Nicola's dad had collapsed on a sofa, his head tipped back, twitching violently each time he snored.

"She said it's Shimlara," yelled Nicola's crazy great-aunt Annie over the music, handing the phone over to her. "I said it was a bit late to be calling. She said it was lunchtime on her planet. Her *planet*! What a jokester!"

Nicola took the phone from Great-Aunt Annie, who marched off, muttering and shaking her head. *When will they start believing that I actually do know people from other planets?* she wondered. After all, it had been international news when Nicola and her friends saved Earth from being destroyed by a spoiled princess from the planet of Globagaskar.

Why would Shimlara be calling Nicola now? It had only been a matter of hours since they had dropped her back home after their last mission.

Nicola's older brother, Sean, appeared by Nicola's side. "Why is Shimlara calling you?"

"How would I know?" said Nicola, irritably, because she was worried.

They went down Grammy's hallway toward her bedroom, where it was quiet.

"Hello? Shimlara?"

"Oh, *Nicola*!" Shimlara's voice sounded tiny and strange, and then she burst into tears. Nicola made an alarmed face at Sean. It wasn't like Shimlara to cry for no reason.

"What's the matter? What's happened?"

"Mom and Dad and Squid have *vanished*!" sobbed Shimlara.

"But are you sure?" said Nicola. "Maybe they went shopping and forgot to leave a note." Her own family was constantly doing that.

"There *is* a note," said Shimlara. Her voice became stronger. "In Dad's handwriting. It says, 'Help, Shiml—'

and then nothing else, as if he was interrupted. I think they've been *kidnapped*!"

"Have you called the police?" asked Nicola.

"What are police?" said Shimlara.

Maybe they had a different name for the police force on Globagaskar. "Who do you call when someone commits a crime?"

"We don't have crime on Globagaskar. We're far too advanced for that. That only happens on prehistoric planets. No offense."

"Okay, but isn't kidnapping a crime?"

"Stop being so picky!" snapped Shimlara. "All I know is that I've got a very bad feeling. Can you and the Space Brigade come to Globagaskar? Please?"

"We're on our way, Shimlara." Sean said, leaning close to the phone.

Nicola gritted her teeth. She was the leader of the Space Brigade. It was *her* job to say dramatic things like that.

"We'll be there as soon as we can," said Nicola. "Just try and stay calm."

"Hurry," said Shimlara. "Please hurry." She hung up.

Sean looked at Nicola, his eyes shining. "Looks like we're going back into space sooner than we thought."

"It looks like it," agreed Nicola. She was suddenly feeling very wide awake.

XCEPT IT WASN'T THAT EASY. HOW WERE THEY
going to get away from Grammy's party? How
were they going to call the other members of
the Space Brigade at this time of night? Furious
parents would refuse to wake their children up.
If Nicola and Sean tried to tell them about Shimlara's predicament, they would say reasonably, "Why doesn't she
call the police?"

"Nicola! Sean! Get out of the way!"

Nicola and Sean's mother raced past, pursued by her
sister, their auntie Peg.

"Aha!" Their mom reached the bedroom at the end of
the hallway first.

"You *always* get the most comfortable bed!" sulked
Auntie Peg.

"What's going on?" asked Nicola.

"We're all staying the night here," said their mother.
"Grammy wants the party to continue on till breakfast
time. You kids are all going to sleep in sleeping bags in the
living room. That will be fun, won't it?"

Oh, yes, great fun, sharing a room with a dozen wriggling

cousins. However, it would certainly be *convenient* for a discreet trip into space.

"Did you win?" Their dad came down the hallway, rubbing his eyes.

"Sure did!" said their mother. Nicola and Sean winced as their parents gave each other high fives.

"See you kids in the morning!" said their mother.

"If we're not around for breakfast it's because we've gone to the pool," said Nicola, trying to buy more time.

"As long as you're back by ten—"

"Of course," said Nicola, crossing her fingers that they'd be back by then. Luckily Tyler always flew their spaceship on Time-Squeeze speed, which meant that they could spend days on another planet, but only a few hours would pass on Earth.

"We can text Greta," she said to Sean, as they closed the door on their embarrassing parents, who were bouncing around on the four-poster bed. "But what about the others?"

Greta was the only one in the Space Brigade who owned a cell phone. (She was also the least popular member of the Brigade, but now that they'd been on two missions with her, it was impossible to imagine leaving her behind.)

"Greta can go and knock on Tyler's window," said Sean. Tyler lived across the street from Greta. "I don't know what to do about Katie."

"Wait a sec," said Nicola. "Katie's mom is away at the moment!" Katie's mom didn't miss a thing, but her dad was an eccentric scientist who wrote textbooks about frogs. "I bet Mr. Hobbs won't even notice we're calling so late!"

Nicola was right. Katie's father was delighted to hear from her. "Nicola! How are you? Still tap dancing?" Nicola and Katie had last done a tap-dancing class when they were five years old.

"You bet, Mr. Hobbs! Is Katie there?"

"I think she might be asleep, but I guess I should wake her. Shouldn't she be getting ready for school?"

"Absolutely!" No need to mention it was past midnight on a Friday.

A minute later she was talking to a sleepy Katie. In the meantime, Sean was busy using a cousin's phone to text Greta.

After Nicola hung up with Katie, Sean read out loud a text message reply from Greta:

Very disorganized as usual, but okay, I'll collect Tyler and see you asap.

"How could we be *organized* for something unexpected like this?" said Nicola.

Sean shrugged. He never let Greta's snarky comments bother him.

"How was Katie?"

"As soon as she heard Shimlara needed us, she didn't ask questions," said Nicola.

Twenty minutes later, the Space Brigade gathered quietly in the front yard of Nicola and Sean's great-grandmother's house. They were whispering because most of the party guests and Grammy had finally gone to bed.

"You didn't forget the spaceship, did you, Tyler?" said Nicola.

"You're dealing with a professional here." The lenses of Tyler's glasses glinted in the moonlight. He pointed to the familiar silver briefcase with the words MINI EASY-RIDE SPACESHIP stamped discreetly on the side. He'd strapped it to the back of his bike.

"I was nervous riding my bike over in the dark," said Katie, trying to smooth down her glossy brown hair where it was sticking up in the back. Nicola had to laugh when she thought of what Katie had been through on their last mission. Maybe it was easier to be brave on a planet other than your own.

"If this turns out to be a wild goose chase, I won't be impressed," said Greta. You wouldn't have thought she'd been in bed when they called. She looked as neat as a pin. "Sometimes Shimlara can be a bit of a drama queen."

This was true, but Nicola immediately jumped to her defense.

"She wouldn't be dragging us all the way to the other side of the galaxy if it wasn't an emergency."

"Okay, guys, stand back." Tyler picked up the briefcase. He pressed a button marked ACTIVATE on the side. As usual, nothing happened for just long enough for Greta to snap, "Is it broken?" Then, suddenly, it began spinning rapidly, until it was nothing but a streak of whirling color. Within seconds, the briefcase had been transformed into a compact, but impressive-looking, spaceship.

"Wha dat?" said a voice.

Nicola spun around.

It was their youngest cousin, Jessie. She was wearing pink pajamas and staring with wide eyes at the spaceship.

"Go back inside, Jessie," said Nicola, in what she thought was a firm, kindly parental voice.

"No," said Jessie in an equally firm, kindly voice. "Wha *dat*?"

"It's a spaceship," said Sean. "Now scoot off, kiddo."

Tyler unlocked the spaceship. The glass bubble on top hinged back and a ladder slid down to the ground.

"Jessie come for a ride!" Jessie's voice rose to alarming levels.

"Can't you control her?" said Greta to Nicola. "Isn't she, like, a *relative* of yours?"

Nicola shrugged. She had no idea how to handle naughty

children except to just give them whatever they wanted. Katie bent down beside Jessie. She was good with children because she had four very naughty little brothers.

"If you quietly go back inside, we'll bring you back something really special from our trip," said Katie. "Would you like something pink or yellow?"

Jessie put her finger to her lip. "Ummm, I think, pink. No, yellow. Pink!"

"I don't think you should bribe her," said Greta. "She'll get unrealistic expectations about life. Do as you're told and go inside, little girl."

Jessie stomped her feet and screamed, "No!"

A light went on inside the house.

"We'd better hurry," said Sean.

"What's going on out there?" called out a voice from inside.

Frizzle, thought Nicola. (*Frizzle* was the Berry family's own private swear word.)

"Go, go, go!" she said. The Space Brigade began scrambling up the spaceship ladder.

Jessie screamed like both her legs had been broken. "Me come, too!"

"We'll bring you back something pink, honey!" Katie ran to the ladder.

Jessie got a firm grip on the hem of Nicola's dress. (She

was wearing a floaty, floral summer party dress to please Grammy.)

The front door of the house swung open.

"Oh, please let go, Jessie," begged Nicola. She staggered to the spaceship with the little girl dragging along the grass behind her.

"Prepare for blastoff," said Tyler.

Nicola's foot was on the second rung of the ladder. Jessie was clutching her leg with both fat little hands.

A voice from the front porch said, "What in the world . . . ?"

Jessie's grip loosened. Sean and Katie leaned out of the spaceship and pulled Nicola inside. She strapped herself into her passenger pod. Through the glass bubble lid of the spaceship she could see her crazy great-aunt Annie striding across the front lawn toward Jessie, her mouth moving rapidly. Nicola couldn't hear what she was saying, but she had a feeling it wasn't "Have a great trip in space, kids!"

Tyler twisted around to look at her with questioning eyebrows.

"Blast off *now*!" she ordered him.

He didn't even need to look back at the controls. He slammed one fist against the big red button.

3

HE SPACESHIP SHOT UP LIKE A FIRECRACKER.
Nicola peered down and saw her crazy great-
aunt Annie scoop Jessie into her arms and point a
warning finger into the sky that Nicola was pretty
sure meant "I'm going straight inside to wake your
parents." Poor Mom and Dad, snoozing happily away in
their comfy bed.

Then Grammy's house, street, and suburb melted away
into a patchwork quilt of glimmering lights. Seconds later
they could see the massive curve of Earth's surface.

"I've never felt so unprepared for a mission." Nicola
gestured at her pretty dress and held up empty palms.

"It's not like you were fantastically prepared for the
other missions," said Greta.

"Luckily, your genius of a big brother is prepared." Sean
grinned smugly and held up a backpack. "Guess what's in
here?"

"Your dirty old sneakers?" guessed Nicola.

Sean opened the bag and pulled out a long, gold-
wrapped chocolate bar that was instantly familiar.

"ShobbleChoc," breathed Katie.

Their last mission had been to the planet of Shobble, home of the most exquisitely delicious chocolate in the galaxy. Sean handed around bars and everyone took huge bites.

"I've also got the Micro Mirth Missiles," said Sean. "We just throw them at our enemies and they'll go weak with laughter."

The people of Shobble had been so grateful for the Space Brigade's help overthrowing an evil commander in chief, they had presented them with a treasure chest full of chocolate and weapons.

"Why did you have the backpack with you at Grammy's party?" asked Nicola. (She wished *she'd* been the one with the chocolate and weapons. It would have made her look so capable.)

"I've been taking it everywhere I go," said Sean. "Just in case."

"At least we've all got our buttons," said Katie. She pulled at a large shiny gold button hanging around her neck.

The people of Shobble had also given each of them a "limited edition gold button," telling them it had "unusual functions you might appreciate one day." Katie had threaded each button onto a thin chain and they had all agreed to wear the buttons around their necks at all times. The buttons had become like Space Brigade membership badges.

"Pity we don't have any idea what they do," said Greta. "If anything."

"We'll find out one day," said Nicola.

"I've been thinking about Georgio and Mully," said Katie thoughtfully.

Georgio and Mully were Shimlara's parents. Everyone in the Space Brigade was fond of them. Georgio was a zany university professor with a huge mustache, who was full of enthusiasm for anything and everything. Mully was lovely and full of surprises (for example, she was an ex-officer of the Globagaskar army). They appeared pretty much like normal parents except for the fact they were close to twelve feet tall. This was because people on Globagaskar were about twice as tall as Earthlings. Even Shimlara's little brother, Squid, who was just three years old, was the same height as Nicola.

"Remember when we picked up Shimlara before our last mission?" said Katie. "Georgio took a phone call and came back looking all serious. I wonder if that call has something to do with why they've gone missing."

"That's a good point. I'd forgotten about that," said Nicola.

Now Katie was showing her up. Nicola was suddenly filled with insecurity. Maybe she should ask the others if someone else would like to be leader this time? She was about to speak, when Tyler said, "Prepare for landing, folks. That's Globagaskar just to your right."

Goodness. He sounded like he'd been piloting spaceships all his life. Everyone else was becoming more confident with each mission, whereas Nicola appeared to be *losing* confidence.

As the spaceship raced through Globagaskar's glittering outer atmosphere, Nicola caught her first glimpse of the planet's two suns radiating beams of cherry-colored light across majestic snowcapped mountain ranges. She remembered her first trip into space, after Georgio had picked *her* as the Earthling Ambassador.

Now Georgio was in trouble and he needed her help. Nicola took a deep, bracing breath. This was no time for insecurity. This was a time for *action*.

After Tyler deftly landed the spaceship in the Gorgioskio backyard, they all went inside to look for Shimlara.

As they walked into the strange, futuristic house with its circular rooms, confusing murals, and unfamiliar technology, Nicola realized she'd never been there before without the whole family. It seemed like any minute Georgio would surely come bounding down the hallway, or Mully would appear offering them cookies the size of dinner plates, or that Squid would run in, his security blanket clutched close, his thumb in his mouth.

But this time the house was eerily silent.

"I hope Shimlara hasn't disappeared now, too," said Nicola, as she pushed open the door of Shimlara's bedroom and found it empty. She realized her heart was beating fast.

She walked into Georgio and Mully's room. Nothing. A curtain rippled in the breeze from an open window. Nicola shivered.

Next was Squid's room. There was someone curled up in his bed.

It was Shimlara. She had pulled her knees to her chest and was cuddling Squid's ragged old blue blanket. Her face was puffy from crying. Her long dark curly hair was a tangled mess. When she saw the Space Brigade all gathered at the bedroom door, she sat up and carefully adjusted the gold button hanging around her neck.

"Please help me find them," she said.

4

IRST SHIMLARA SHOWED THEM WHAT SHE'D discovered so far.

There was the tray bobbing around in the pool with the half-drunk cups of tea and a cookie with a single bite taken from it. "Dad would never leave an almond cookie like that," said Shimlara. "Unless something really terrible happened to interrupt him."

There was the piece of torn notepaper Shimlara had found lying in the backyard, in Georgio's handwriting. It said, *Help, Shiml*—as if he'd been interrupted.

There was the fact that the Gorgioskios' aero-car was still sitting in the garage.

And there was Squid's security blanket, which was really the most compelling evidence of all.

"They don't go anywhere without Squid's blanket," said Shimlara.

"Maybe your parents decided it was time he grew out of it," said Greta. Shimlara just stared Greta down until she muttered, "Or maybe not."

Now they were all sitting around the Gorgioskio dining-room table, trying desperately to think of what to do next.

"I've called every single person Mom and Dad know," said Shimlara. "None of them have any ideas. One of Dad's friends at the university muttered something like, 'I *told* him not to get involved.' When I asked him what he meant, he hung up."

"I wonder if—" said Nicola. She stopped, trying to piece her thoughts together. She was thinking about the circumstances that had led to her first meeting the Gorgioskio family. The king and queen of Globagaskar had gone on vacation, leaving their daughter, Princess Petronella, in charge. Unfortunately, Princess Petronella had taken it upon herself to turn Earth into a giant garbage can. That's when Georgio and Mully set up the Save the Little Earthlings Committee.

"Maybe Georgio and Mully are trying to help another planet," said Nicola. "Like they helped Earth. Have they talked about anything like that lately?"

"They're *always* trying to help other planets. I zone out. I'm not really into current affairs. They go on about *injustice*. It's so boring." Shimlara suddenly looked embarrassed. "Although of course it wasn't boring when they were trying to save Earth. That was different. That was really interesting."

"Your parents are good people," said Katie to Shimlara. "They're an inspiration!"

Shimlara nodded miserably. "They even won this award for 'Services to the Galaxy' from the United Aunts." She pointed out a big gold plaque hanging on the wall, engraved with Georgio and Mully's names. "It's a really big deal."

"Who are the United Aunts?" asked Nicola.

"It's a universal organization of wise aunts," explained Shimlara. "There are representative aunts from every planet. Their goal is to 'encourage peace and love and good manners throughout the galaxy.'"

"It must be like the United Nations on Earth," said Tyler. "Except, um, with aunts."

"Mom and Dad were so thrilled to get to shake hands with the aunts," said Shimlara. "I should have been more excited for them. I was saying, 'Who cares about some boring old aunts?' And they were so excited for me just because I won third place in a spelling bee!"

"Maybe your parents keep some paperwork about the different causes they're involved with?" suggested Nicola, anxious to change the subject as Shimlara was looking so upset and guilty.

Shimlara stood and they all looked up at her. When she was sitting down, Nicola forgot that Shimlara was as tall as a basketball player. It gave her a start. Yet on Globagaskar, Shimlara was the shortest girl in her class.

"Dad has a file he calls the Outrage File," said Shimlara. "It's filled with newspaper clippings. Mom won't let him read it after ten p.m. because he gets himself into such a state he can't sleep. I'll get it. Maybe there will be some clues."

She left the room. Sean looked longingly at the gold hutch sitting in the middle of the table. It was a common Globagaskarian appliance called the Telepathy Chef. You used mental telepathy to order the food you wanted.

"Maybe we could get the Telepathy Chef to make us some pizza," said Sean.

"It might not be polite," said Katie regretfully.

"Shimlara won't mind," said Sean.

He closed his eyes. They all watched him lick his lips as he presumably thought hard about pizza. He opened his eyes and pressed the button on the Telepathy Hutch. Seconds later, a tray slid out.

"That doesn't even look *edible*," said Greta.

It was a dish of what appeared to be snowballs sprinkled with grass clippings.

"Were you thinking about snow?" asked Nicola.

"No! I was thinking about how the best pizza we'd ever had was on the planet of Shobble, on that snowy mountain—" Sean stopped. "Okay, maybe I thought *briefly* about snow!"

"Were you thinking about grass clippings, too?" said Tyler.

"*No!* I was thinking about a pizza I had one day after I mowed—"

"The lawn," finished Katie.

Sean banged his forehead against the table. "That machine is *faulty*."

Shimlara walked back in lugging an enormous file brimming with newspaper clippings.

"Oh, sorry, are you guys hungry?" she said. "What's that supposed to be?"

"Pizza," answered Nicola.

Shimlara blinked once and pressed the button on the Telepathy Chef. Three trays slid out in quick succession, each containing a delicious-looking pizza.

"How did you do that?" asked Sean.

"You've just got to focus," said Shimlara. "Now, speaking of focusing, do you think we could focus on finding my family?"

"Sorry," said everyone guiltily, as they all avoided one another's eyes and helped themselves to slices of pizza.

"Hey!" said Sean suddenly, with his mouth full of pizza. "You know how you can read minds on Globagaskar?"

"Yes," said Shimlara.

The people of Globagaskar were able to read minds and project their voices into other people's brains. Fortunately, it was considered bad manners to read someone else's mind except in dire circumstances.

"Well, why don't you just read your mom or dad's mind and find out where they are!" said Sean, obviously thrilled with his own genius.

Shimlara rolled her eyes. "Do you think I wouldn't have done that already if it was possible? You need to be able to see someone's face before you can read their mind."

"Just a thought," said Sean, deflated.

Shimlara put the file she was holding on the table. "Everyone take a few clippings and see what you can find."

Nicola grabbed a handful and spread them out in front of her. She read:

PLANET OF GROON BANS ALL FORMS OF SMILING

King of Groon speaks his mind: "What can I say? Smiles bug me."

FLOODS ON PLANET OF ARTH

Arth-Creatures may be extinct if nothing is done, states Environmental Czar.

VOLCOMANIA DECLARES WAR ON THE PLANET OF WHIMSY

"The planet of Whimsy must be taught a lesson!" thunders President Mania.

PLANET OF DUMPWOOD BANS REFUGEES FROM GROON

"It's not our problem they're not allowed to smile on their stupid planet," proclaims Prime Minister.

Oh dear. There were so many planets that needed help. How could they possibly work out which one had taken Georgio and Mully's interest?

Nicola took another bite of her (perfect) pizza, and the name Gorgioskio caught her eye on one of the clippings.

She read quickly.

LOCAL RESIDENTS FIGHT FOR GROON'S RIGHT TO SMILE!

Georgio and Mully Gorgioskio have started a new committee called Save the Smile on Groon. They have sent a petition to the king of Groon. The king's response was swift: "Mind your own beeswax."

"Listen to this!" she went to say to the others, but Tyler got in first.

"I've got it!" He began to read from one of the clippings. *"Intergalactic activists Georgio and Mully are at it again. This time they're taking on the planet of Finbat, where the government has decided to only allow workers a day off once every three years. 'This is an absolute outrage,' said Mully Gorgioskio. 'We've started a committee called Help Finbat's Overworked Workers.'"*

Tyler looked up from his article. "Maybe their disappearance has got something to do with the government of Finbat."

"But listen to this!" said Katie. *"This time those well-meaning Gorgioskios have gone too far. They have started a committee called Save the Arth-Creatures. Arth-Creatures are deadly, ugly, ill-mannered creatures that love nothing more than snacking on tasty humans. Yet the Gorgioskios are bent on saving them. 'We should do everything in our power to stop the extinction of any species,' bleated bleeding heart Mully Gorgioskio. This journalist's humble opinion: Save the Arth-Creatures by feeding them two tasty morsels: Georgio and Mully Gorgioskio."*

"That's an awful thing to say," said Shimlara, her voice shaking. "You don't think that journalist has—"

"Of course not," said Nicola. "The journalist was trying to be funny."

"Your parents have got so many causes," said Sean. "They're like superheroes of the galaxy!" He paused. "Except without the superpowers."

"Yeah, they're great, although I'm not sure it's absolutely necessary to save the Arth-Creatures," said Greta. "They tried to eat *us*!"

"Anyway," said Nicola decisively. "This isn't getting us anywhere. All we've learned from this is that your parents are involved with a *lot* of different causes."

"So what next?" said Shimlara. "Do we just give up?"

"No way!" said Nicola. "We don't give up. We—" She searched her mind desperately for something they could do next.

She was interrupted by a sound from outside the house. They all looked at one another.

"Maybe the kidnappers have come back to get me," said Shimlara.

Suddenly she leaped to her feet.

"Come and get me, whoever you are!" she yelled. "I don't care! I'm in—"

Sean jumped up on a chair so he was high enough to slap his hand over her mouth. "You can't help your family if you're kidnapped, too!"

Shimlara's eyes rolled around angrily, but she nodded, pushing away his hand.

There was definitely something going on outside the house. It sounded like footsteps. Actually, it sounded like an army of footsteps.

"Where are those Micro Mirth Missiles?" whispered Nicola to Sean.

Sean quickly pulled out a pack of miniature rocket-shaped objects from his backpack and opened it up. He handed a missile to each person. "Just pull on the wire at the back and throw."

There was an enormous crash. A gust of air rushed through the house.

"I think they've kicked down the front door," whispered Shimlara.

There was the sound of heavy boots running through the house. Nicola swallowed a scream as she and the Space Brigade stood up and backed themselves up against a wall, their Micro Missiles held aloft.

Suddenly the room was filled with giant men dressed entirely in black.

5

THROW YOUR MISSILES!" SHOUTED NICOLA.

Her hands shook as she pulled the wire from her own missile and threw it hard at the intruders. It bounced off one of the men's elbows. He glanced down and frowned.

The rest of the Space Brigade threw their missiles at almost the same time. The missiles didn't explode. They rolled harmlessly around on the floor. There was no smoke. Nicola saw one of the men kick curiously at one of the missiles with the side of his big black boot.

Were they broken? Had they ever worked?

There was silence. It was bizarre. The giant men weren't doing anything. They stood very still, as if at attention, their chests inflated, their faces like granite.

The Space Brigade huddled together, staring up at them.

The men stared back.

And then suddenly, amazingly, Nicola saw their mouths begin to twitch. Broad smiles crept across their faces.

They're making fun of us, thought Nicola.

The men began to choke and sputter, their huge shoulders shaking, as if they were kids trying not to giggle in class.

A gale of laughter swept the room. The men were overcome with it. Tears of joy slid down their red, scrunched-up faces. One by one, their knees buckled and they fell to the floor, shaking all over with laughter.

They think we're ridiculous, thought Nicola bitterly.

She watched one of them crawl over to a Mirth Missile, examine it, and then throw back his head and laugh even harder, as if he'd never see anything so funny in his entire life. Suddenly she thought, *You fool! They're not laughing at us! They're laughing because the Mirth Missiles have WORKED!*

Nicola turned to tell the others that now that the intruders were disabled by laughter, it was time to escape, but before she had a chance to speak, she was struck by just how extremely funny it was that she'd thought the intruders were laughing at them.

She began to giggle helplessly. She saw the rest of the Space Brigade was laughing, too. Shimlara pressed her fists hard into her cheeks. Tyler and Sean seemed to have turned to jelly and were trying to hold each other up. Greta and Katie were pointing at each other and laughing hysterically.

Oh dear, thought Nicola, *the Mirth Missiles are affecting us, too. They're useless weapons! Which, when you think about it, is pretty funny.*

Nicola found herself lying on the floor, roaring with

laughter. Next to her one of the intruders was facedown, hitting the floor with his fist as he cackled.

Suddenly a cranky voice boomed across the room. "WHAT IN THE WORLD IS GOING ON HERE?"

It was a familiar voice.

Nicola lifted her head.

A girl was standing in the middle of the room, her hands on her hips, looking disgusted. She was wearing a beautiful green satin dress with gold embroidery, although Nicola noticed one of the sleeves was carelessly ripped. A tiara sat lopsided on her curly red hair.

"Princess—" said Nicola. She was laughing so hard she could hardly get the words out. "Princess Petronella."

"What's so funny?" demanded the princess.

The laughing continued.

"Do I have food in my teeth?" The princess pulled off her tiara and held it up to her face, grimacing at her reflection. This caused a fresh gale of laughter.

"*What?*" Princess Petronella stamped her foot in frustration. "Just tell me what's so funny!"

Nobody answered. They were too busy laughing. But Nicola could feel the funniness seeping away.

Sure it was funny, but it wasn't hilarious.

The shrieks of laughter were replaced by sniggers and snickers, chuckles and chortles.

Actually, it wasn't even that funny at all.

The effect of the Mirth Missiles was wearing off.

The room became silent, except for the sound of people clearing their throats. Slowly everyone got to their feet, shamefaced and avoiding one another's eyes.

"My sincere apologies, Princess Petronella," said one of the men. "They attacked us with Mirth Missiles. Those weapons should be banned. They destroy dignity like *that*!"

He snapped his fingers to demonstrate and looked accusingly at the Space Brigade.

"Well, excuse *me*, but you were the ones knocking down our front door!" responded Shimlara.

"Yes, I am, ah, regretful, about that," said Princess Petronella. (Nicola remembered how horrified Princess Petronella's parents had been when they heard her use the word *sorry*. Apparently Globagaskarian royalty weren't meant to use language like that.) "Mom and Dad insisted I bring along the palace guards. The guards think that's how you open doors—by kicking them down."

"Is there another way?" said a confused voice from the back of the room.

"Why are you here, Princess Petronella?" said Shimlara.

"Just a moment," said Princess Petronella. She clapped her hands. "Guards! Wait for me outside!"

The room emptied in seconds. It was like a forest had suddenly cleared.

"They frightened us to death," said Nicola. "We thought they were here to kidnap us. You see, Shimlara's parents and little brother have gone missing and—"

"I know they've gone missing," interrupted Princess Petronella.

"You do?" said Shimlara.

"Of course. That's why I'm here."

**O YOU KNOW WHERE THEY ARE?" ASKED** Shimlara desperately.

"We think we do," said the princess.

"They're alive, then? You know they're alive?"

"We *believe* they're alive," said the princess. "Look, we're going to explain everything. That's why I'm here. To bring you back to the palace."

She turned to Nicola. "It's good to see you little Earthlings again! Have you been enjoying the Earth oceans that I saved for you?"

"You didn't *save* our oceans!" protested Sean. "We convinced you not to destroy Earth."

"Details, details!" said the princess airily.

"Also, we don't just swim all day long," said Greta. "We have our educations to consider. We go to school. We have homework. Extracurricular activities."

The princess ignored Greta. She was busy looking out the back window at the Gorgioskio backyard. "Speaking of swimming, should we have a dip before we go? The palace pool must be twenty times the size of yours. I'd love to try a teeny pool!"

"I think Shimlara might be in a hurry to find out about her parents," said Katie.

"Oh." The princess looked disappointed. Nicola could see her struggle. She was so used to getting her own way.

"Well, all right," she said ungraciously. "I guess we can go now. After all, you are all my *friends*. Friends make sacrifices for one another, don't they?"

"That's right," said Katie encouragingly.

"Excellent! I adore friendship! So now Shimlara owes me one sacrifice! Should we record that somewhere?" said the princess.

"How are we getting to the palace?" interrupted Tyler.

"Why, the Royal Aero-Carriage, of course," said the princess.

"Why, of *course*," said Sean. "What a stupid question, Tyler!"

Tyler grinned and the princess smiled uncertainly at the two boys. She sometimes had a hard time following Earthling humor.

"Yes indeed! Ha ha!" Then her smile vanished. "Go outside to the front of the house where the carriage is waiting. All of you. Now."

They all went outside (past the palace guards on their hands and knees attempting to fix Shimlara's front door) to find an enormous, intricately carved carriage floating in midair in front of the Gorgioskio house.

"It's so beautiful," breathed Katie.

"It's actually becoming quite shabby," sighed Princess Petronella. She stepped forward and a staircase carpeted in red velvet sprang out from the carriage door. "Follow me," she ordered.

They walked up the elegant royal staircase.

The inside of the carriage looked like a sitting room in a palace. "Oh, yes, this is *very* shabby," said Sean dryly.

"Do you really need to have your own throne when you travel?" Sean pointed at the three thrones. "Would it hurt you to sit on a couch for five minutes?"

"I don't understand the question," said the princess.

"Don't worry about it," muttered Sean.

"We're moving," marveled Tyler. He'd gone to stand at one of the windows. "And there's no turbulence at all."

The princess ignored him.

"Can you at least give me an idea of where my family is?" asked Shimlara.

"I'd really prefer to talk about myself!" said the princess brightly. "I want to tell you everything! Well, let's see, I've been doing kickboxing lessons, and I—"

"I don't think it's fair to Shimlara to make her wait," interrupted Nicola.

"Oh," said the princess. She frowned. "Well, all *right*!

That's two favors you owe me now, Shimlara! Why don't I sit on my throne and you can all sit at my feet while I explain."

"I'm not sitting at your *feet*," said Greta disgustedly.

"Why don't we all sit on these comfy couches," said Katie.

"I guess I could do that," said Princess Petronella. She sat down tentatively on a plush velvet lounge. "Actually, this is quite comfortable! How fascinating!"

Shimlara's voice suddenly spoke up loud and clear in Nicola's head.

If she doesn't tell me soon, I'm going to strangle her scrawny neck!

Nicola glanced at Shimlara and saw that she was sitting in the seat opposite the princess, her hands demurely folded, her eyes downcast.

Be careful. She might read your mind, thought Nicola.

She wouldn't be bothered to read my mind! She's too busy thinking about herself! I forgot how selfish she is! She's a spoiled—

"Shimlara," said Princess Petronella. "We believe your parents and brother are being held captive somewhere on the planet of Whimsy."

Shimlara looked startled. "Where? What do you mean, 'held captive'?"

Mmmm, maybe she was reading my mind, she said in Nicola's head.

"One of Georgio's newspaper clippings mentioned the planet of Whimsy," said Nicola. "Some other planet declared war on it."

"That's right," said the princess. "The planet of Volcomania has invaded the planet of Whimsy."

"Let me guess," said Sean. "Shimlara's parents started a committee."

"They did," agreed Princess Petronella. "The Stop the Wicked War on the Planet of Whimsy Committee. They've been organizing petitions, protest marches—that sort of thing. Your parents are very *passionate* people, aren't they?"

"Was it the Volcomanian government who took them?" asked Shimlara.

"Our spies believe so," said Princess Petronella.

"Oh, why couldn't they just take up some sort of boring hobby like normal parents!" said Shimlara.

"This is outrageous! I assume the Globagaskarian royal family is going to demand they be returned!" said Greta.

"Unfortunately we can't confront them about it," said Princess Petronella. "Because we'd have to admit we spy on them, and then they might declare war on *us*."

"But someone has to do something!" Katie chimed in.

"Of course," said the princess. "That's why I came to get you." She looked up. Nicola followed her gaze and saw the glistening jewel-encrusted spires of the Rainbow Palace against a backdrop of snow-draped mountains. Nicola had barely been aware that they were moving.

"We're here," said the princess. She stood up and straightened her tiara. "The Chief of Special Intelligence is waiting to speak to you all."

She paused and looked down at Shimlara.

"I did mention that I took up kickboxing, didn't I, Shimlara? And that I excel at it? So I don't recommend your attempt to 'strangle my scrawny neck.'"

7

THE SPACE BRIGADE SAT AROUND A LONG OVAL table in the Rainbow Palace. At one end of the table were Princess Petronella and her parents, the king and queen of Globagaskar, sitting on elaborate thrones.

The king and queen gave the Brigade slightly frosty nods of welcome.

The last time they'd met, the princess's parents had been threatening to throw them all in jail for kidnapping their daughter.

At the other end of the table was the Chief of Special Intelligence: a woman with a short brown haircut in the shape of a bowl. She was dressed in a dark uniform with rows of medals across her chest.

Her name was XYZ40. Apparently all members of Special Intelligence were referred to only by their code names.

"Where is the leader of the Space Brigade?" asked XYZ40. She seemed to be looking around as if someone were missing.

Nicola coughed nervously and lifted her finger. "That would be me."

"Right," said XYZ40. She frowned, looking at Nicola's pretty party dress. "And this is the same Space Brigade that just completed a mission where you helped overthrow the dictator of the planet of Shobble?"

"That's us!" said Nicola cheerfully. It was nice to be reminded of their previous successes.

"I see." XYZ40 studied them all. "You seem very young."

"Good skincare," said Sean, giving the Space Brigade a secret wink. "We don't look our age."

"Really?" XYZ40 stroked her cheek. "How extraordinary."

"Shall we begin?" said the queen of Globagaskar. "It's just that your mention of skincare reminded me that I have a very important facial after this meeting."

"Yes, and I urgently require a nap," yawned the king.

"Of course, your majesties," said XYZ40. "Let me begin with some background for the Earthlings."

A white screen slid down behind her. She picked up a long pointer.

"This is the planet of Volcomania."

The screen filled with a dark, fiery landscape.

"Volcomania's most significant geographical feature is its volcanoes," said XYZ40. "The exact number of live volcanoes on the planet has never been confirmed; however, it's estimated that a volcano erupts every two and a half minutes. This obviously makes life difficult, due to the constant danger of being splattered with boiling lava. As a result, the planet's inhabitants have gradually evolved an unusual, tough, scaly skin."

The screen showed a picture of a family: a man, woman, and two children. They would have looked perfectly normal, except for their skin. It was a deep red in color and ridged like a crocodile's.

"I really must *not* miss that facial," murmured the queen.

"To avoid third-degree burns, visitors must wear a specially formulated lava screen," said XYZ40. She handed around small tubes that looked like sunscreen. Nicola examined hers. It said: FACTOR 25,000,000 LAVA SCREEN. *To avoid potentially fatal lava burn, apply to ALL exposed skin, hair, AND clothing.*

Goodness. Nicola thought about how she often missed a patch of skin when she was applying sunscreen.

"Are they able to grow any crops on Volcomania?" asked Tyler. He always asked the intelligent questions.

"No, the quality of the soil makes it impossible to grow any food on the planet," said XYZ40. "All food is imported from other planets. Volcomania's main source of income is manufacturing goods from solidified lava. For example, this happens to be a Volcomanian vase."

She lifted a squat brown vase from the table and smashed it hard against the side of the table. It didn't break.

"Volcomanian goods are impossible to break," said XYZ40. "Their biggest customers are families with small children and people with bad tempers. If you're having an argument and you want to throw a teacup, you can do so without fear of it breaking. For example . . ."

She put down her pointer, picked up a nearby teacup and threw it against the wall. It shattered into tiny fragments.

"Oh!" XYZ40's hands flew to her mouth. "I am sorry, your majesties, I was absolutely positive that was a Volcomanian teacup."

"It was actually a priceless heirloom," sighed the queen. Flustered, XYZ40 picked up her pointer again.

"The nearest planet to Volcomania is the planet of Whimsy. In fact, the planets are actually joined."

A picture of two planets appeared on the screen. One was large and the other small.

"This is Volcomania." XYZ40 indicated the larger planet. "It is joined to the planet of Whimsy here." She pointed to a long, thin cylinder attaching the two planets. It was like both planets had been stuck on either end of a toothpick. "This is actually an Underground Sea. The only way to travel between the two planets is via this sea."

She pointed to a pale pink halo around the planet of

Whimsy. "It is impossible to land a spaceship on Whimsy because of this atmospheric dust. Although deceptively pretty, it's actually Choker Dust. It causes spaceships to choke up and disintegrate."

"So I guess the only way you can get to the planet of Whimsy is by first landing on Volcomania and then scuba diving through the Underground Sea?" said Greta.

"Exactly," said XYZ40.

Oh my, thought Nicola.

"And that's where Mom and Dad and Squid are?" said Shimlara.

"We'll get to that," said XYZ40. "First I want to brief you on the planet of Whimsy."

The king yawned enormously. "Surely they know all about Whimsy? What are they teaching them in school these days?"

XYZ40 cleared her throat. "Ah, your majesty, apart from Shimlara, the members of the Space Brigade are Earthlings. It's my understanding that most Earthlings have little or no awareness of the existence of life on other planets."

"Silly creatures," said the king.

"The planet of Whimsy is quite a different kettle of fish from Volcomania," said XYZ40. A picture of an exquisite lake appeared on the screen.

"I won't belabor the point, but it's simply the most beautiful planet in the universe." XYZ40 clicked through a number of pictures, each one more stunning than the last. Nicola felt like her eyes were being assaulted by beauty. She couldn't describe the feeling it gave her. It was like she'd just listened to a type of music she'd never heard before and it had touched her soul.

"Ah," moaned Nicola and Katie at the same time, as the last slide disappeared.

XYZ40 narrowed her eyes at them. "I see that you two are susceptible to Whimsy's beauty. Arty types, are you?" She said the word *arty* as if it were something vaguely disgusting.

"I like to write stories sometimes," admitted Nicola.

"I play the cello a little," said Katie. (Nicola knew she was being modest. Katie was actually a very talented cellist, although she was shy about performing in public.)

"You two will have to be extra careful on Whimsy," said XYZ40.

"So we're going to Whimsy, then?" said Shimlara. "To rescue my family?"

"I am getting to that," said XYZ40.

A new slide appeared on the screen. It showed a group of people lying in a meadow. They all had long wispy hair, rosy faces, and dreamy expressions. Some of them were holding flowers. Others were staring in blissful wonder at the sky.

"The people of Whimsy are the most artistic in the universe," said XYZ40. "The landscape seems to inspire them. They write symphonies and plays. They paint. They sculpt. They sing. They're really very talented. Unfortunately, they're also somewhat . . ."

"Hopeless," supplied the king.

"Yes," admitted XYZ40. "They're incredibly absent-minded. They're not at all practical. They don't grow crops even though the soil would be perfect for it, and they have no business sense whatsoever. They're always running out of food, and sending messages to Volcomania asking for urgent supplies. Up until now, the Volcomanian government has put up with this. In fact, being an entrepreneurial type of people, they've tended to exploit it. In return for supplying bread and milk, they demand that the Whimsians hand over their paintings or sculptures. Then they sell them around the galaxy for huge profits."

"I've said it before and I'll say it again, those Whimsians all need to be packed off to business school," said the king.

"I think I remember Mom and Dad talking about a Whimsian painting that's now worth a billion bars of gold," said Shimlara. "The person who painted it sold it to a Volcomanian for a *ham sandwich.*"

"So why has Volcomania declared war on the planet of Whimsy?" asked Tyler. "It seems like they've got a pretty good arrangement going."

"Volcomania has a new president," said XYZ40. A picture appeared on the screen of a Volcomanian woman in a crisp business suit. If it wasn't for her scaly skin, she might have been quite attractive.

"Mrs. Mary Ellen Mania," said XYZ40. "After winning the presidency, Mrs. Mania gave a very persuasive speech about how the planet of Whimsy was actually part of Volcomanian territory and should be under their rule. She sent in the troops the following week. Once Whimsy surrenders and is under Volcomanian rule, she wants the people to work in artistic factories where they'll have a certain quota of paintings or symphonies to produce every week. They'll receive a wage and according to Mrs. Mania, they can 'finally start to act like grown-ups.' No more lying around in meadows staring at the sky. Also, they'll have to start farming on the weekends."

"Oh, those poor people," said Katie.

"Is the planet of Whimsy fighting back?" asked Sean.

"Well, they're very upset but, the thing is, they're not actually very good at war. They don't have an army.

In fact, they didn't even have a president. They'd forgotten to reelect one after the last president resigned. When the war began, they very hurriedly put this man in charge."

A picture appeared of a fair-haired man wearing a beret and a paint-splattered smock.

"This is Henry Sweet," said XYZ40. "He's a very good artist, but a terrible president. Not surprisingly, Volcomania is currently winning the War on Whimsy. The only reason they haven't managed to wrap it up in under a week is because of the time it takes to transport weapons, troops, and provisions through the Underground Sea. They've had to leave many of their bigger cannons and tanks behind because they can't fit them through the sea. Here is some of the damage the Volcomanian army has done so far."

Picture after picture of terrible sights appeared on the screen.

A meadow of flowers crushed by the heavy black boots of the Volcomanian army.

Beautiful sculptures riddled with bullet holes.

A family lying facedown on the ground, their hands over their heads, while their home burned behind them.

A young girl sobbing over the burned remains of her harp.

"No wonder my parents are trying to help!" said Shimlara passionately. She turned to the king and queen. "Why aren't *you* helping the planet of Whimsy?"

"Oh, my dear, we have expressed our grave concern over Volcomania's actions," said the queen. "Every planet's government has written a strongly worded letter to Mrs. Mania. I composed our letter myself. It took me a whole *hour*. I was exhausted, as you can imagine. People don't appreciate how much work goes into being a royal."

"Why hasn't Globagaskar declared war on Volcomania?" asked Greta.

"Obviously, you wouldn't understand this as a commoner and an Earthling, but that's how galaxy wars begin," said Princess Petronella condescendingly. "This is all much more *complicated* than you realize!"

"Surely the United Aunts isn't happy about this!" said Shimlara.

"The United Aunts has been loudly condemning Volcomania's actions," said XYZ40. "They're extremely upset. In fact, they were about to hold a press conference an hour ago on the matter, but it was canceled at the last minute."

"Perhaps the United Aunts has been kidnapped, too," said Shimlara.

XYZ40 looked shocked. "Don't be ridiculous. Something must have come up! Or perhaps the aunts are sick. They are quite elderly."

"How could *all* of them be sick at the same time?" said Shimlara quietly.

"It does seem a little mysterious," admitted XYZ40. "But no planet would dare kidnap the aunts!"

"So basically you are doing nothing about this war," said Sean.

The king yawned. "I really do need my nap."

The queen caressed her face. "My skin is just crying out for that facial!"

Only Princess Petronella looked at all concerned.

"We're not doing nothing," she said. "I'm going to make a diplomatic visit to Mrs. Mania's son and try to speak some sense into him. Even though he's a horrible toad of a boy and it will be *very* boring."

"But what about Shimlara's family?" asked Nicola.

"The Gorgioskios are fine citizens," said XYZ40. "It's true they can be a little, well, annoying, at times with all their 'causes,' but we obviously want to help them. We considered sending in our own rescue team, but all our best agents are busy at the moment with a rather tricky problem we're currently experiencing on the planet of Me—"

She stopped and bit her lip.

"Anyway, the point is, we felt there was another option."

"That's where you come in," said Princess Petronella.

The Space Brigade had all turned to stare at her.

"We're going to smuggle you into Volcomania so you can go to Whimsy and rescue them!"

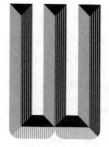**HAT DO YOU MEAN BY 'SMUGGLE'?"**
asked Sean. *He's probably hoping there'll be some rappelling involved,* thought Nicola.

"We're going to have to parachute you in," said XYZ40.

Oh great. Sean grinned. Katie sighed.

"Why?" said Nicola. She didn't think parachuting over live volcanoes was the most sensible idea.

"The Volcomanians are being very careful about who they let onto the planet at the moment," said XYZ40. "You would be recognized by the Secret Service. The Space Brigade is starting to build quite an intergalactic reputation . . ."

"Really?" said Nicola.

"Us?" said Tyler.

"Are you sure?" said Katie.

"Like, we're famous?" said Greta.

"That's so cool," said Sean.

"I mean, I knew word was getting around the galaxy," said Shimlara excitedly. "But I didn't think—"

"Could we get back to the subject at hand?" said XYZ40 firmly.

The Space Brigade snapped back to attention.

"As a royal visitor, Princess Petronella won't be under much scrutiny," said XYZ40. "So we should be able to parachute you out of the royal spaceship quite easily. You'll be met by one of our secret agents on Volcomania. His code name is JJ-11. He'll identify himself with the phrase 'Lovely day for a stroll.' You must respond, 'I do enjoy a piece of rhubarb pie.' He'll arrange a transport and secret undercover identities for you."

"Okay," said Nicola. "And what happens after that?"

"I assume with your experience, you'll have no problem scuba diving through the Underground Sea to Whimsy and then tracking down the prisoners? Of course, Whimsy is a war zone, so you'll have to be careful, but you've probably been through many a war zone in your time, right?"

XYZ40 looked at Nicola.

"No problem at all," croaked Nicola. Shouldn't war zones be *avoided*?

The king and queen were fidgeting on their thrones. "You don't need us for all the details, do you?" said the king.

The queen stood up. "I'm afraid I really need to go for my facial," she said. "I owe it to my subjects to keep my skin flawless." She gave Princess Petronella a kiss on the cheek. "Darling, have a wonderful time in Volcomania!"

"Mom!" said Princess Petronella. "I'm doing this to try and help stop the war. It won't be *fun*. I can't stand Mrs. Mania's son!"

"Oh, now, you make sure you play nicely with the little fellow," said the king, ruffling Princess Petronella's hair.

"Dad!" The princess readjusted her tiara. "I'm not going on a playdate. I'm going on a *diplomatic mission*."

"Of course you are, sweetie," said the king. He stood up and yawned. "I'm off for my nap." Then he and the queen swept out of the room. A moment later, the queen popped her head back through the door and trilled, "I nearly forgot! Good luck, Space Brigade! I *do* hope none of you die!"

She vanished.

Princess Petronella's face was bright red. "They are just . . . *impossible*!"

XYZ40 spent the next few hours giving the Space Brigade detailed instructions about meeting places, geography, history, secret agents, and code words, by the end of which Nicola felt like she'd spent two weeks stuck in a classroom.

Finally XYZ40 consulted her clipboard. "I think that's everything. I'll just give you your kits."

She handed each member of the Space Brigade a back-pack.

"It contains your parachute, lava goggles, extra tubes of lava screen, two-way radios, binoculars—that sort of thing," said XYZ40.

"Where's my backpack?" said the princess.

"But, your highness, you won't be parachuting," said XYZ40. "You'll be—"

"Playing nicely with the toad," finished the princess sulkily.

"Your highness, let me assure you that your role is absolutely crucial," said XYZ40. "For one thing, we wouldn't be able to smuggle in the Space Brigade if we didn't have the excuse of the royal visit, and for another, you may actually have some luck convincing the toad, I mean, Mrs. Mania's son, to influence his mother."

"Don't worry about it," said the princess. "I'm used to a life without fun or interest."

"Thank you for your help, Princess Petronella," said Shimlara humbly. "This is very nice of you. You're a great friend."

"It sure is nice of you," agreed Nicola. Actually, now that she thought about it, it was a bit odd that the princess was being so generous with her time.

The princess beamed. "I am an incredibly nice friend,

aren't I? And I'm also giving up important study time with a new tutor. He's a galaxy-famous mathematics genius and he was going to give me a weeklong workshop on 'The Fine Art of Multiplication.' Unfortunately I'm going to have to miss it now! And he's not available for another five years!"

Aha. So, it wasn't just helping out Shimlara's parents that was motivating the princess! She was getting out of studying math! That made more sense. The Space Brigade smiled at one another, while the princess pondered, "Perhaps I should write a book one day—*The Seven Secrets of Friendship*."

There was a crackling sound and XYZ40 turned away from them, pressed a hand to her ear, and listened carefully. She was obviously wearing some sort of two-way radio earpiece. "Roger that," she said crisply.

She dropped her hand. "The Royal Spaceship is ready."

It was early evening and Nicola had her face pressed to the Royal Spaceship window, ready for her first glimpse of the planet of Volcomania.

It was amazing to Nicola that this spaceship was even airborne. It was a small city! It had its own bowling alley, a movie theater, and a giant swimming pool the size of a football stadium.

Instead of the cramped pods on Tyler's Mini Easy-Ride Spaceship, passengers reclined on full-length velvet sofas. Staff was available to rub your feet, but Princess Petronella was the only one taking advantage of this service. The others were all too nervous about what lay ahead of them.

They had all slathered themselves, their hair, and their clothes in lava screen and strapped their parachutes to their backs. Fortunately, the parachutes seemed quite simple to operate, with a PULL HERE! tag on the rip cord. Nicola's hand hovered near it.

"Just don't pull it until you've *jumped*," said Tyler, from the sofa next to Nicola.

Nicola moved her hand away. "Of course not."

"I see the volcanoes!" said Sean.

Nicola looked out and saw explosions of fiery red on the planet below. She could also see the tiny planet of Whimsy with its halo of pink dust attached to Volcomania by the long tube that Nicola knew was the Underground Sea. She shivered as she imagined scuba diving through it. She liked swimming, but she didn't particularly like diving underwater for too long. Of course, it wasn't like she'd have to hold her breath the whole time, but still.

As the spaceship got closer to Volcomania, they got a clearer view of the volcanoes and the red molten lava exploding from each one, like rows of bubbling cooking pots. Nicola imagined how just one drop would sear her skin. She took out her lava screen and began to reapply a fresh new layer. She saw the rest of the Space Brigade doing the same.

"A little harder, please," said the princess sleepily to the poor servant who was rubbing her feet. Apparently, the president's family lived in a specially constructed Lava Protection Bubble so she didn't have to worry about applying lava screen.

"Can the Space Brigade please assemble at Exit Door Five Hundred and prepare for drop-off," said a polite voice over a loudspeaker.

Nicola's heart jumped like a crazy gymnast. She packed her lava screen into her backpack and stood up, wondering if her own face looked as terrified as the others. They were all adjusting their parachutes with trembling fingers.

"Shouldn't we have had some *training* before suddenly jumping out of a spaceship wearing a parachute?" said Greta to Nicola, as if Nicola had any control over the situation.

"Parachuting is *easy*!" Princess Petronella sat up so abruptly, her foot-rubbing servant toppled backward onto the floor. "I once spent a delightful week parachuting on the planet of Bliss."

"Did you have any training?" asked Katie, helping the servant back to her feet.

"Of course! I spent a month working with my own personal parachute trainer," said the princess. "He had me land on a specially built soft surface until I got my technique right. He said I would have broken my legs otherwise." She laughed merrily. "Ah, good times."

The Space Brigade looked at her with stony faces.

"Oh," said the princess. "Well, I'm sure you'll all be fine. Just remember to bend your legs when you land."

"Space Brigade report to Exit Door Five Hundred right NOW!" said a rather less polite voice over the loudspeaker.

"Have fun," said the princess, lying back down and presenting her feet to the servant. "Please don't worry about me, stuck with the boring toad. I'll manage. Royals are used to making sacrifices."

"Is she for *real*?" said Sean, as the Space Brigade ran down the corridor along the side of the spaceship.

Nicola was busy looking at the numbers on the exit doors. "Oh, no—that's only Exit Door Twenty! We're so far away!"

They all picked up the pace, their parachutes bouncing on their backs.

"Are you all deaf? Space Brigade to Exit Door Five Hundred!" said the loudspeaker voice.

"We're *coming*!" called Nicola.

The corridor seemed endless. It was like something

out of a nightmare. By the time they got to Exit Door Five Hundred, they'd all be so exhausted they'd just fall out.

With her longer legs, Shimlara was the fastest. She ran ahead of them, calling out the numbers on the doors.

Finally, she shouted triumphantly, "Exit Door Five Hundred!"

The rest of the Space Brigade ran up behind her, their faces red and sweaty, their chests heaving.

Exit Door Five Hundred was wide open and the heat and noise from the erupting volcanoes below struck them like a brutal slap across the face.

Nicola peered out at the fiery landscape below.

I can't, she thought. *I cannot jump out of this spaceship.* She could feel her own resistance as massive and immovable as a wall of concrete in front of her.

"I can't do it," said Katie to Nicola in a quiet, terrified voice.

"Space Brigade! You are required to jump on the count of three," said the voice over the loudspeaker. (Nicola was starting to hate that voice.)

"One . . . ," boomed the voice.

Shimlara was clinging to the side of the Exit Door.

"We have to do it," she said, except you could tell she was facing the same concrete wall of resistance as Nicola.

"Yes," said Sean unconvincingly.

Nicola darted a look at her brother. His face was white. He was the one who *loved* doing this sort of crazy stuff! If Sean was scared, what hope did the rest of them have?

"We need training," insisted Greta.

"Maybe there is another way we could get to Volcomania," said Tyler.

"Two . . . ," said the voice.

Nicola's mind was filled with images.

She saw Georgio performing his celebratory chicken dance the first day she'd ever met him when he'd turned up in her classroom and picked *her* as the Earthling Ambassador.

She saw Mully bending down to put her hand on Nicola's shoulder and saying, "I have complete confidence in you."

She saw Squid, dragging his blue blanket along behind him, his thumb jammed in his mouth.

If it wasn't for Georgio and Mully, Earth would no longer exist. Nicola's planet would be a garbage dump. They had to help the Gorgioskios.

"Three!" shouted the voice over the loudspeaker.

When you're frightened of something, Nicola's mother had once said to her, *there's only one way to make the fear go away— and that's to do the thing that's frightening you. You just have to ignore the fear and DO IT, the faster the better!*

Nicola looked at the others, their faces illuminated by the fiery light of the exploding volcanoes.

She pulled her lava goggles over her eyes.

If she didn't jump, the others never would.

She didn't let her mind think anymore.

She just jumped.

9

...R...I...Z...Z...L...E! THAT
was the word like a long, silent scream in Nicola's mind as she plummeted through the night sky toward the volcanoes below, hot air blasting her face, a roaring sound in her ears. She wasn't floating on her stomach in a neat star shape like the parachutists she'd seen on television. She was flailing about, her hands clawing at the air, as if she could hold on to something, or somehow climb back onto the spaceship.

Rip cord.

She needed to pull her rip cord.

She grabbed at her shoulder and felt nothing. Panic exploded in her chest. She felt again, and there it was. She pulled.

There was an enormous tugging sensation, as if a giant had grabbed her by the shoulders and wrenched her upright.

The roaring sound stopped abruptly like a switch had been turned off. She looked up. Her parachute was purple silk, rippling silently above her. She was safe. Her dress fluttered around her legs. Mmmm, her dress and parachute matched quite well. What a strange sight she must have made, parachuting above volcanoes in the middle of the night dressed for a birthday party.

Nicola could see Sean, Shimlara, and Tyler, not far behind her. Their parachutes had all opened and they were all smiling with the same blissful relief that Nicola felt.

Katie and Greta had only just jumped. The Royal Spaceship was flying off into the distance behind them.

To Nicola's chagrin, she saw that Greta looked like an absolute skydiving professional. She was floating in a star shape and, as Nicola watched, she calmly reached for her rip cord and her parachute opened.

Katie, on the other hand, looked much like Nicola had probably looked. She was tumbling crazily through the air, arms and legs in every direction.

Okay, pull your rip cord now, thought Nicola.

Katie kept falling.

Nicola could hear a faint, eerie sound that she thought might have been Katie's scream.

Pull your rip cord. Katie, please, please pull your rip cord.

Katie continued to fall like someone pushed from the side of the cliff. She flew past Nicola. Nicola saw only a flash of gaping mouth and bulging eyes.

"Katie, pull your rip cord, you silly, silly . . . !" screamed

Nicola and she'd never heard her own voice sound like that: violent with terror.

She could hear the rest of the Space Brigade screaming at Katie, too, and just when she thought she was about to see her best friend die right in front of her, Katie's parachute burst open like a blossoming flower. It was quite possibly the most beautiful thing Nicola had ever seen.

Nicola's eyes filled with tears. She was going to be very angry with Katie when they landed.

Landing. Right. That was the next thing to accomplish.

XYZ40 had told them that the Royal Spaceship would drop them as close as possible to a red hut with 3A on the roof that would be easy to spot from the air.

"The Volcomanians color-code everything," she'd said. "It makes it quite convenient to get around. Of course, you'll find it's quite a different story when you get to the planet of Whimsy."

Nicola looked down beneath her. It didn't matter that it was the middle of the night because the constant explosions from the volcanoes lit up the landscape like daylight. Everywhere she looked she could see erupting volcanoes.

It was quite beautiful in a frightening sort of way.

Goodness! Was that a *city* perched on the side of that volcano? Nicola tried to imagine living her daily life on the side of an active volcano.

She suddenly remembered her teacher, Mrs. Zucchini, telling them about an ancient city in Italy that had been buried under ash after a volcano erupted. The city was called Pompeii, and when Mount Vesuvius erupted, the ash preserved everything—even the bodies. The city was frozen forever like a time capsule. Apparently you could still see the terrified expressions on some of the dead victims' faces.

Why wasn't the entire planet of Volcomania buried in ash? Nicola wished she'd remembered Pompeii when XYZ40 was briefing them. She could have asked her.

As her parachute sank lower, she could feel the heat radiating from the volcanoes like a million summer days. Beads of sweat formed on her forehead.

Was the lava screen waterproof? What if she sweated it all away? What if her skin became as red and scaly as a Volcomanian? What if . . .

"I can see the hut!"

It was Katie's voice.

Oh! Nicola had forgotten all about the hut. She'd just been letting her parachute and mind drift.

Nicola looked down and saw a small, squat, red hut with 3A clearly marked on the top.

She reached for the toggles that Tyler had told them would steer the parachute. ("How do you know this?" Greta had asked. "I don't know," Tyler had answered. "I just do.")

Nicola pulled the left toggle and the parachute gently floated down to the left. She pulled right and it floated down to the right. It was quite fun. Maybe she'd take up parachuting as a hobby when she got back to Earth.

She zigzagged through the air toward the hut and saw with horror that it seemed to be right next to the crater of a permanently erupting volcano. It was like a pot of milk boiling over on the stove. Except it wasn't milk—it was lava.

Couldn't XYZ40 have picked a landing spot that wasn't quite so close to a volcano crater? They would have to parachute straight through a *fountain* of lava.

"It's going to burn us!" screamed Greta.

"We're wearing lava screen!" Nicola shouted back. "We'll be fine!" She hoped. Her parachute sank lower and suddenly it was raining fire. Nicola recoiled and shut her eyes as glowing droplets fell onto her skin and dress. But there was no burning sensation. The droplets of molten lava felt as cool as raindrops and slid painlessly off her. She opened her eyes again. Thank goodness for lava screen.

"Nicola!" said Tyler. "We forgot—" His parachute floated near hers and then floated off again in a gust of wind.

"What?" Nicola called back.

She could smell something sizzling. It was like cloth burning. She looked down at her dress. No. It was fine. Tyler's parachute hovered near Nicola's again.

"We forgot the parachutes!" he cried.

What did he mean? They had their parachutes!

Nicola laughed and pointed at Tyler's parachute. "No, we didn't!"

And then suddenly she understood. Tyler's parachute was dotted with dozens of smoldering holes from the showering lava.

"We forgot to put lava screen on the parachutes!" cried Tyler.

ICOLA! WE FORGOT TO—"

Shimlara plummeted past Nicola, pointing frantically at the burning holes in her own parachute.

"Yes, I *know*," Nicola called back. Did they really expect her to come up with a SOLUTION to this disaster?

Boom!

The volcano directly below them erupted with a huge explosion that lit up the sky. Nicola gasped as she was completely drenched in lava. She wiped off her face with both hands—imagine if she'd forgotten to lava screen her face!—and looked up at her parachute.

It was burning; crackling flames were shooting up into the sky.

There was a *whoosh* sound and her parachute collapsed inward.

Someone shouted, "Nicola! We forgot to—"

But Nicola never heard the rest because suddenly she was falling much too fast toward the planet below.

Cough!

Splutter!

Eeeeuww-cough!

Nicola spat and spat again, trying desperately to clear her throat of the most horrible taste. She seemed to have swallowed an entire bucket of . . . something disgusting. It had a burned, ashy taste.

She opened her eyes and the first thing she saw was a huge furry gray creature with white teeth looming over her.

Nicola screamed and backed away.

"Calm down," said the furry creature. "It's me."

Nicola blinked.

It was Shimlara. She was completely covered in some sort of gray, ashy material, so only her eyes and teeth were visible.

Nicola looked down at herself and realized she was covered in the same stuff. Her dress was ruined. She tugged at the charred remains of her parachute dangling uselessly behind her back.

"I think we've landed face-first on a mountain of volcanic ash," said Shimlara huskily. "I've got some lodged right at the back of my throat."

"What about the others?" said Nicola.

She stood up and her feet sank into the ash as if she were standing on a sandy beach. Another ash-covered figure appeared in the distance, choking and coughing. It was her brother. She could tell by the careless way he was swatting at the ash on his clothes.

"Over here, Sean!" she called.

Sean jumped, yelled, and held up his arms in a defensive karate position.

Nicola giggled. "It's us! Nicola and Shimlara!"

Sean dropped his arms and called out, "Yeah, yeah, I knew that!"

He stomped through the ash toward them, and there was a shout of terror as he nearly stepped on Tyler.

At the same moment, Greta and Katie emerged from the ash, screaming when they saw each other, and then screaming more in response to the other's screams.

Finally, everybody calmed down and stood in a circle, brushing ash off their clothes and hair, and tearing off the burned remains of their parachutes.

"How could you have forgotten lava screen for the parachutes?" said Greta to Nicola. "We really need checklists. That's what I'd do if I were the leader. I would have checklists for *everything*."

Nicola managed not to say, "Well, why didn't *you* remember lava screen?" She'd learned that the best way to respond to Greta's criticism was to ignore her. Instead she said, "Oh, look at those giant fans! I was wondering what happens to the ash from the volcanoes!"

She pointed to a row of fans as big as windmills on the side of the volcano. They were efficiently blowing the ash and cinders from the volcanoes into the mountain of ash that they'd landed upon.

"XYZ40 told us about the fans," said Tyler.

"Did she?" said Nicola. "I don't remember that part."

"You were thinking about the lava screen and remembering a time you forgot to put sunscreen on at the beach and everybody at school called you tomato face," said Shimlara.

"Shimlara!" said Nicola, embarrassed. "Why were you reading my mind? That's private! That's so rude!"

"Sorry." Shimlara looked down and kicked at the ash. "I was just wondering what you were thinking about."

"You should have been concentrating on XYZ40's briefing, Nicola," said Greta. "I mean if you're thinking about *sunburn* at such an important time, you really have to ask yourself, are you the right person for the job?"

"Oh, be *quiet*, Greta!" snapped Nicola, because the thing about criticism was that it always stung the most when it was true.

"Well!" said Katie brightly. "What next?"

"Now we have to get off this mountain of ash," said Sean. He ducked as the nearby volcano erupted again, showering them with lava.

"And maybe we should reapply our lava screen," said Shimlara. "I'm sweating."

They all were. The heat from the erupting volcanoes was intense. It seemed to suck the air from Nicola's lungs.

They all pulled out their lava screen tubes from their backpacks and pasted thick layers across their faces.

Nicola walked over to the edge of the ash mountain. "It's going to take us ages to walk down."

"I was thinking we could sit on bits of parachute and *slide* down to the bottom," said Tyler.

"Good idea! That'll be fun!" Sean examined the remains of his parachute.

"This mission isn't about fun," said Greta primly. "There is a terrible war going on. And we're here to find Shimlara's family."

"I don't think my family would mind if we have some fun along the way," said Shimlara. "In fact, Dad would encourage it."

Nicola didn't say anything. She was still recovering from Greta's earlier comment.

A short time later, they were all sitting on pieces of parachute silk on the edge of the mountain of ash.

"Last one down is a rotten egg!" said Sean, and he slid off.

I bet he didn't like it that I was the first one to parachute out of the spaceship, thought Nicola and grinned to herself. As the big brother, he was always supposed to be first.

"It probably killed him that you jumped first," said Shimlara, who was sitting next to Nicola.

"*Shimlara!* You've got to stop reading my mind!" said Nicola.

"I didn't!" protested Shimlara.

"Mmmmm," said Nicola distrustfully.

"Cross my nose," said Shimlara, and carefully drew a little cross over her nose with the tip of her finger.

"On Earth we say 'cross my heart,'" said Nicola.

Shimlara giggled. "Really? How funny! Why would you cross your heart?"

"Why would you cross your nose?"

But Shimlara had already pushed off the edge, shouting, "Last one down is a rotten Earthling!"

Nicola watched her go. It was only her and Katie left.

"Remember how we loved playing on the slide at the park?" said Katie. She and Nicola had known each other ever since they were babies. There was an embarrassing photo at Katie's house of the two of them sitting together in a sandbox wearing nothing but diapers.

"I remember." Nicola grinned.

"One, two, *three*!" said Nicola and Katie at the same time, and they slid off.

A cool breeze blew against Nicola's hot, sweaty face as she slid smoothly down the side of the ash mountain, her legs stuck out in front of her.

Suddenly all her childhood memories of sliding came back to her in a rush. She could feel that familiar mix of exhilaration and fear. She could see her dad's face at the bottom of the slide, his arms out wide, ready to catch her.

Except this was the *ultimate* slide experience. It was faster, longer. She could hear the other members of the Space Brigade crying out silly things like "Whooeeee!"

Greta would probably be highly disapproving.

Oh, who cares what Greta thinks?

Nicola lifted her arms up straight in the air and shouted, *"Whoo hoo!"*

THE **SPACE BRIGADE LANDED AT THE BOTTOM OF** the mountain of ash in a shrieking, breathless tangle of arms and legs. They were all laughing hysterically, almost delirious from the excitement of the slide. Even Greta was giggling.

"Ahem," said a serious, deep voice.

Nicola was still chortling as she sat up. Then she abruptly stopped laughing as she looked up at a very tall, very bald man standing in front of them, his hands on his hips, an extremely disapproving, raised-eyebrow, pursed-lip expression on his long, pale face.

"Lovely day for a stroll," he snapped.

What an odd thing to say, thought Nicola.

"Nicola!" hissed Sean. "That's the code phrase!"

Of course! She'd quite forgotten they were being met by a Globagaskarian secret agent. And now Nicola was supposed to say something back to identify herself. What was it? Finally, it came to her.

"I do enjoy a piece of pie."

The man stared at her blankly.

"Oh, erm, I mean, I do enjoy a piece of rhubarb pie,"

said Nicola hurriedly. Really! Who came up with these ridiculous code phrases? They didn't even make sense.

The man dropped his hands from his hips. There was an expression of pure disbelief on his face.

"I'm Agent JJ-11. So *you're* the highly trained Space Brigade?" he said.

"That's us." Nicola felt fraudulent, as if she and her friends were all just pretending to be the Space Brigade.

JJ-11 looked around him, as if for an audience who could share his consternation. Finally, he gave a resigned shrug. "Well, if you'd like to follow me, I've arranged accommodation for the evening, transport, and fake identities for you."

The Space Brigade stood up, trying to brush away the ash from their clothes and the leftover smiles from their faces.

JJ-11 went striding off and they all had to run to keep up with him.

"Imagine living here," said Katie, as they followed JJ-11 up a steep, winding track around the bottom of the volcano. She gestured at the fiery explosions from the volcanoes and the dark, brooding city in the distance. "It would be like living in a nightmare."

"In regard to your secret identities," said JJ-11, "I decided the safest thing would be for you to pretend to be a news crew from Earth reporting on the progress of the war. I've set you up with various props—press passes, microphones, notepads, cameras, et cetera. You'll need to appear as authentic as possible. You'll be pleased to hear that I've arranged for some genuine Earthling transportation for you. A wealthy Globagaskarian once picked up this motorized conveyance as a souvenir while vacationing on Earth. It fits perfectly with your identities." He couldn't hide the note of pride in his voice.

"Must be some sort of jeep," said Tyler quietly.

They rounded a corner and JJ-11 gestured in front of him at a very, very familiar sight. "Your transportation."

"Well, how ridiculous!" said Greta.

Sean snorted.

"What is it?" said Shimlara uncomprehendingly.

"It's a bus," said Nicola.

"It's a *school* bus," said Greta. "How *embarrassing*. We're not going to look like traveling journalists. We're going to look like . . . schoolkids!"

Nicola refrained from pointing out that they were, in fact, schoolkids.

JJ-11 didn't seem to have heard their comments. He was walking alongside the bus, running his hand along the paintwork.

"It's a strange, wonderful machine," he said. "The engineering is delightfully basic." He turned to look at them.

"I assume this is the sort of vehicle Earthling journalists would use?"

"Erm, possibly," said Nicola. It seemed unlikely that anyone on Volcomania would recognize it as a school bus, and she didn't want to irritate JJ-11 any further.

"These are the *keys*," said JJ-11, handing Nicola a set of keys.

"Thank you," said Nicola.

"Keys," repeated JJ-11. "That's what they're called. You use them to turn on the vehicle."

"Yes," said Nicola. "I'm an Earthling. I know."

"I should think so," snapped JJ-11.

Goodness. He really was a difficult person.

"This is where you'll sleep tonight," said JJ-11. He indicated a small stone hut they hadn't noticed while they'd been looking at the bus. "You'll find food and drink inside, and all your props, passports, and clothing."

"You've done a great job," said Katie to JJ-11. "It must have been a lot of work setting all this up for us."

JJ-11 looked startled. Suddenly he smiled and his sour face was transformed.

"Well, yes, it was a lot of work, but that's my job, so I obviously don't begrudge . . . but certainly, yes, it took some time . . . and, ah, I do like to do things properly, but of course any professional does, but, ah . . . !" He clapped his hands together and his smile vanished. "Any questions?"

"What about scuba diving gear for when we go through the Underground Sea?" asked Sean. Nicola shivered. Sean was obviously looking forward to that part.

"On the conveyance." JJ-11 jerked his head at the bus.

"What about maps?" asked Tyler.

"No need for maps on Volcomania," said JJ-11. "Follow the Blue-5 road. All the way to the Underground Sea. Once you get to Whimsy, you'll just have to ask people for directions. Not that anybody will give you any. They'll just recite poetry, or stare into your eyes for twenty minutes without saying a word. The Whimsian personality is somewhat frustrating." JJ-11 gave an irritated grimace at the thought of the Whimsian personality.

"Any more questions?" he barked, as if they were all annoying Whimsians.

Nicola could think of lots of questions. *Where does the Blue-5 road begin? How will we find Georgio and Mully once we get to Whimsy? How safe is that scuba diving equipment?*

But she could see JJ-11 trying to hide a yawn. He obviously wanted to get back to his own bed.

"No, that's all," she said. She tried to follow Katie's example by sounding grateful and polite. "Thank you very much for your help."

JJ-11 ignored her. For some reason, Nicola never got the same response as Katie did when she tried to be nice to unpleasant people. Perhaps they could tell she was faking.

"Good night then," said JJ-11. He suddenly bent over and shook each of their hands vigorously. "Good luck." Then he turned around and vanished off into the dark, fiery night.

Nicola and the rest of the Space Brigade looked at one another. Their shoulders were slumped and their filthy, ashy faces suddenly looked deflated and weary. Nobody said a word as they followed Nicola inside the stone hut—exhausted and drained.

What would tomorrow bring?

12

NICOLA'S MOTHER WAS RIGHT: EVERYTHING did seem better the next day. ("One day," Nicola's mother had once said, "you will realize that I am right about *everything*." This day had not yet come. For example, her belief that Nicola looked so much "prettier" with her hair pulled out of her eyes was plainly, demonstrably wrong.)

Light was pouring through the windows of the stone hut. There wasn't much inside except for a row of stretcher beds, where the Space Brigade had collapsed last night. Nicola couldn't even remember putting her head on the pillow.

She hopped out of bed and walked to one of the windows. As usual, she was the first one up. The rest of the Space Brigade was still sound asleep.

Nicola opened the window and leaned out, eager to see what Volcomania looked like in the daylight.

The first thing she noticed was the sky.

So far, in her space travels, Nicola had experienced four planets.

The planet of Earth had one sun.

The planet of Globagaskar had two cherry-colored suns.

The planet of Shobble had one sun.

The planet of Arth had—she couldn't remember, she'd been too busy trying to avoid being eaten by Arth-Creatures.

And now, here she was on a planet with not one, not two, but dozens of tiny fiercely glowing orange suns. The sky looked busy, like it had been decorated with balloons for a party.

The suns lit up the landscape with a harsh orange glow. The volcanoes were still erupting regularly, but the lava didn't seem as molten red as it had during the night. Or perhaps she was just getting used to it. The sound of the eruptions was starting to seem as ordinary as the sound of waves crashing on a beach.

Nicola yawned and turned away from the window.

"Good morning," whispered Tyler. He was sitting up in bed, peering short-sightedly at Nicola. "I can't see who you are but I would bet a million dollars you're Nicola." He reached for his glasses sitting next to his bed, put them on, and smiled when he saw he was right. "Knew it. You owe me a million dollars."

"Ha," said Nicola. "Let's find breakfast!"

Tyler hopped out of bed and together they explored the hut until they found a small kitchen. There was a pile of boxes on the table.

Tyler picked up one and read out the label: *"Bapples: imported from the planet of Plenty."*

He opened it up to reveal an unfamiliar fruit that looked like banana-shaped apples.

"All the food is imported from other planets," said Nicola, as she looked through the boxes.

"That's because they can't grow any food here," said Tyler. "Remember? Oh, look—this box is imported from Earth! It says *oggs*. Have you ever eaten oggs?"

They tore open the box.

"Eggs," said Nicola. "They got the name wrong."

"Excellent," said Tyler. "I can make scrambled eggs."

Suddenly another box caught Nicola's eye.

"Is that what I think it is?" said Nicola. "Yes, yes, it is! It's *hot ShobbleChoc* from the planet of Shobble!" She opened the box and saw rows of steaming mugs.

"I wonder how they keep it hot during transportation," said Tyler, as he helped himself to a mug, but then he stopped talking and drank. Hot chocolate from Shobble did that to you. It was so blissfully delicious, you couldn't think of anything except hot chocolate.

Half an hour later, the rest of the Space Brigade woke up to find a table set with a white tablecloth, and a strange and wonderful breakfast. There were Tyler's scrambled eggs, together with an array of unrecognizable, imported food from other planets. And of course, next to each plate was a mug of hot ShobbleChoc.

"Well done, you guys," said Sean, who was always generous with praise when it came to his stomach.

As they all sat around the table eating their breakfast and listening to the sounds of volcano eruptions, they talked about the day ahead.

"I guess you'll have to drive the bus, Tyler," said Nicola. Tyler was definitely their most qualified person when it came to flying, driving, or even piloting hot-air balloons.

"Yeah," said Tyler. He sounded uncertain.

"If you can fly a spaceship," said Katie, "I'm pretty sure you could drive an ordinary school bus."

"I'm sure I *could* do it," said Tyler. "I've watched our school bus driver and I think I'd be a better driver than him. The only thing is, I don't think my legs will reach the pedals."

"So that means the person with the longest legs will have to drive it," said Greta.

They all turned to look at Shimlara, who was about a head taller than their school bus driver. They were all thinking about the time she had flown them in her helicopter to the Rainbow Palace to kidnap Princess Petronella. It had been a very scary flight.

"Maybe we should all wear crash helmets," said Sean.

Shimlara looked down at her untouched plate of breakfast and her face crumpled. They all stared as tears began to slip down her face.

Sean was horrified. "I was only joking!" Shimlara wasn't normally the sensitive type.

Shimlara took a deep, shaky breath. "It's not you," she said. "I just suddenly remembered that Mom tried to talk to me the other day about the War on Whimsy. She asked if I would like to come along to a meeting. I told her I would rather die and couldn't she talk about something interesting for once? Wasn't that the most horrible thing to say! And now she's been kidnapped and who knows if we'll be able to save her."

"That was a pretty horrible thing to say to your mother," agreed Greta, as if she'd never said anything unkind in her life. "You probably really hurt her feelings."

"Greta!" said Katie. "It's all right, Shimlara. I think mothers are pretty forgiving about things like that. I know my mother is."

As if Katie would ever say anything mean to her mother, thought Nicola. She said out loud, "And we are going to find your family, Shimlara. I guarantee it."

"That's actually pretty irresponsible of you to say, Nicola," said Greta. "I mean, nobody can guarantee that. We've got to go into a war zone and we don't have any idea where they are on the planet of Whimsy. Be honest. This mission is probably doomed."

"Greta!" said everybody at the same time.

"What?" Greta looked around at the cranky expressions on everybody's faces.

Nicola sighed. It was true, she couldn't guarantee they would find the Gorgioskios, but wasn't it better to try to give Shimlara some hope?

She changed the subject. "Well, I guess we should see what clothes JJ-11 left for us to wear. Oh, and we'd better work out our roles."

"What do you mean, roles?" said Sean.

"Well, if we're pretending to be a news crew, then, you know, one of us should be the camera operator, somebody else should look after sound. That sort of thing. Oh, and one of us should be the actual journalist who does the interviewing."

She tried to make the last part sound casual.

Sean grinned. "And I bet *you* want to be the reporter, hey, Nic?"

"Oh, well, not necessarily," said Nicola, although that was exactly the role she wanted. "Maybe it would be better if Shimlara was the journalist, so she could read people's minds."

"It's easier to read minds when you're not asking

questions at the same time," said Shimlara, who seemed to have recovered from her tears. "I'll just be the crazy bus driver."

"I'll be the makeup artist," said Katie cheerfully.

"And I'll be the cameraman," said Tyler.

"I'll do sound," said Sean. "The guy wearing headphones always looks the coolest."

That left Greta and Nicola.

There was a pause. Nicola didn't look at Greta.

"I'll be the *producer,*" announced Greta.

Yes!

"So I guess that leaves you as the reporter," said Katie to Nicola.

"I guess it does," said Nicola nonchalantly. She would be so good at it! She would ask clever, probing questions with a serious, thoughtful expression on her face.

"The producer is the one who organizes everything," said Greta. "So basically I'm in charge of everything. I tell the reporter what to do, what questions to ask, where to stand, who to interview, all that sort of thing."

"Umm, I'm not sure about that," began Nicola. Had she just made a terrible mistake?

"Ah, guys," said Sean. "Remember, we're just *pretending* to be journalists. Don't take your undercover identities too seriously."

"Of course not," said Nicola and Greta hastily.

Katie had left the table and now she returned with her arms full of clothes.

"I found our outfits," she said. "They're fine, except they're a bit big. I think he forgot how short we are compared to Globagaskarians."

She held up some colorfully printed short-sleeved shirts and khaki shorts—the sort of clothes that journalists would wear on assignment somewhere warm and tropical. Not exactly ideal for a war zone, but they would work.

BOOM! BOOM! BOOM!

The Space Brigade put their hands over their ears as three volcanoes all erupted in quick succession.

"How do people live on this planet?" asked Katie, as she dropped her hands.

Nicola stood up. "Let's go meet some Volcomanians and find out."

13

THE SPACE BRIGADE CLIMBED ABOARD THE
school bus, dressed in the clothes JJ-11 had left
for them. Everyone except for Shimlara had rolled
up their sleeves and hems. Naturally they were
all slathered in lava screen from the tops of their
caps to the tips of their toes.

"You don't need to sit all the way back there!" said
Nicola, as she saw Sean automatically heading for the back
seat of the school bus.

"Can't sit anywhere else!" Sean called back without
turning around. "It doesn't feel natural."

Funnily enough, they all seemed to sit in the seats they
would normally sit in if they were going to school. Greta
was at the front, while Katie and Nicola sat next to each
other in the middle of the bus. Only Tyler didn't bother to
sit down. He stood next to Shimlara in the driver's seat,
ready to give her instructions.

Nicola watched him take a firm hold of the pole. "All
right, Shimlara. Turn the key."

The bus engine roared and Nicola and Katie gripped
on tight to the seat in front of them as they lurched off

down the hill away from the hut. "Piece of pie!" called out Shimlara.

"You mean piece of *cake*," corrected Greta.

"Nope!" said Shimlara. "I mean—*whoops*!" Tyler leaned over and helped pull the steering wheel back as the bus nearly veered off the road.

The bus continued at a slower pace, winding down the side of the volcano.

"That looks like a city down there!" called out Greta. Nicola peered out the window and saw a constellation of flickering lights in the distance and what looked like office towers and church steeples silhouetted against the gray sky.

"And there's the Blue-5 road!" shouted Greta, who seemed to have the best spot on the bus.

Nicola could see they were heading toward an orderly intersection with clear, easy-to-read signs indicating roads paved with different-colored bricks. "Blue-5, Blue-5—*not* Red-11!" cried Tyler, grabbing the wheel again from Shimlara.

They made it onto the Blue-5 road and Nicola relaxed. Good. Now they just had to stay on this road until they got to the Underground Sea.

"How about we turn the radio on?" called out Sean. "We can hear some Volcomanian music!"

"Quiet down at the back of the bus!" Tyler called back, in a good imitation of their normal school bus driver, but he reached over and turned a dial. The radio crackled to life. It was a news bulletin. Nicola wasn't especially interested in current affairs on Earth, but it was entirely different when she was on another planet. She leaned forward with interest as a deep, authoritative voice read out the news:

The president, Mrs. Mania, has ordered the drafting of a further ten thousand soldiers for the war on Whimsy. Anyone with a name beginning with N, S, T, M, or L should report immediately for duty at their nearest Draft Office.

In other news, the Volcomanian Army has captured the Whimsian town of Melody. Mrs. Mania said this was an important strategic move for the army. Total surrender by the planet of Whimsy is expected within a matter of days. ("Then why are they drafting more soldiers?" asked Tyler.)

A small group of anti-war protesters is creating traffic chaos on the Blue-5 road, heading south. ("We're heading straight for the chaos," said Greta.) *Police have been called.*

In intergalactic news, there has been no sign of the United Aunts for the last twenty-four hours. Kidnapping is suspected. Mrs. Mania reacted angrily to allegations that

Volcomania was in any way involved. ("Bet they did it!" called out Sean.)

It should be a cool to mild day ("Cool to mild?" exploded Shimlara) *with south to southeasterly breezes and low-level volcanic eruptions throughout the day.*

A cheery DJ's voice came on the radio. *And now turn up your dials for the latest top-ten hit from the Lava-Heads! It's going to rock your socks off, people!*

Everyone winced as a strange sound erupted from the radio like the wails of a badly injured cat. Tyler quickly switched it off.

"Right," said Greta. She stood up and turned around so she was facing the back of the bus. "I think we should pretend to be doing a story on the anti-war protest. That way, we can interview the protesters and we might find some important information to help us find Shimlara's family."

Nicola nearly groaned out loud. This was an excellent idea. Why hadn't she thought of it herself? Now Greta would use it as an opportunity to prove that she should be the leader of the Space Brigade.

"Great idea," said Nicola generously.

"I know," said Greta. She sat down and Nicola breathed a sigh of relief. Maybe this time Greta wasn't going to bother trying to make a point.

Greta stood up again and faced the back of the bus.

"I was just thinking, this really proves that *I* am better qualified to be the leader of—"

"Whoops-a-rosie!" called out Shimlara, as the bus veered off the side of the Blue-5 road, causing Greta to quickly sit down again without finishing her sentence.

Don't worry, Nic, she's never going to be leader of the Space Brigade, said Shimlara's voice loud and clear in Nicola's head.

Katie nudged Nicola and gave her a wink. Although Nicola and Katie couldn't read each other's minds or speak in each other's heads, they'd been friends for long enough that Nicola had a pretty good idea what Katie was thinking. Her loyalty was as solid as lava stone.

Hey, I know you've known Katie forever but my loyalty is just as solid! said the voice of Shimlara in Nicola's head.

SHIMLARA! KINDLY VACATE MY BRAIN! shouted Nicola without moving her lips.

Nicola pulled out a notepad and pen from her backpack. She chewed on the pen as she tried to come up with some excellent questions that would show Greta that she deserved to be the leader.

"Here's the protest!" shouted Tyler. Nicola's notepad flew off her lap and onto the floor of the bus as Shimlara jammed on the brakes.

She looked out the window of the bus and saw a small group of Volcomanians marching along the Blue-5 road, holding placards high above their heads.

At first glance, the Volcomanians could have been mistaken for Earthlings. They were short and tall, thin and fat, fair-haired and brunette. However, as Nicola looked closer, she saw their red, scaly skin and hooded eyes. She shivered slightly. It wasn't their fault their skin had evolved that way, but it had to be said, they weren't the prettiest life-form she'd come across on her intergalactic travels. It didn't help that their clothing was so drab. They all seemed to be wearing dung-colored, loose-fitting shirts and pants.

Katie was reading out loud some of the signs they were carrying.

STOP THE WICKED WAR ON WHIMSY!

VOLCOMANIA, SHAME, SHAME, SHAME!

WHIMSY IS A PLANET OF ART AND SONG, NOT BULLETS AND BOMBS!

DID OUR OWN PRESIDENT ORDER THE KIDNAPPING OF THE UNITED AUNTS?

"Stop the bus!" called out Nicola, anxious to take control before Greta did. Shimlara pulled over to the side of the road and turned off the bus engine. Everyone stood up, looking nervous.

"Remember, you're an Earthling camera crew," said Nicola. "Look confident, aggressive, and sort of nosy. Like real journalists. They just barge their way into any situation. Oh, and make sure you've got your press passes!"

As Nicola said this she checked that she still had her own pass. It was a large gold card hanging on a black cord around her neck. Nicola was grateful to JJ-11 for finding such authentic-looking passes. Wearing it made her almost believe she really was a journalist.

Tyler hoisted a movie camera over his shoulder and Sean picked up the sound equipment. Katie had a beauty case full of makeup, while Nicola had her microphone and notepad. Shimlara jangled the bus keys and Greta officiously tapped her pen against a clipboard.

"I'll do all the talking," announced Greta crisply.

"Ignore her," said Sean in Nicola's ear as they all walked up the aisle and off the bus.

Greta didn't hesitate. She walked straight into the crowd of protesters, holding her press pass high, and shouting, "Press! Press!"

Nicola couldn't help but be impressed. Who cared if she was irritating? It was worth it to have her on the Brigade. Congratulating herself on this mature response, Nicola followed close behind Greta, holding up her press card in the same way.

One of the Volcomanians dropped his PEACE, NOT WAR sign by his side and stuck his face close to Nicola's. She tried not to flinch when she saw his scaly, crocodile skin up close. "You're not Volcomanians. Where are you from?" he growled.

"We're from Earth," stammered Nicola. She'd hoped to sound like a confident journalist but instead her voice came out like a frightened five-year-old.

She cleared her throat.

"We're an Earthling news crew," she said firmly. "We're here to interview you about the War on Whimsy. Are you prepared to answer a few questions?"

Now she sounded pleasingly aggressive. The Volcomanian actually looked nervous.

"On camera? Me? On TV?" he said and bit his lip. "Oh, I don't know. I might say the wrong things. You'd be better talking to my wife. She always has a lot to say." He grabbed for the sleeve of a woman marching next to him. "Bertha! This is a journalist from Earth! She wants to interview you!" His wife, who had what looked like peace symbols painted on her red, scaly cheeks and was shaking an instrument that looked like a tambourine, was shouting at the top of her lungs, "*Peace*, not *war*, *hear* me *roar*!" She turned around and saw Nicola and the rest of the Space Brigade.

"A journalist from Earth! That funny little planet! But don't you think you're the only planet in the galaxy?"

"We wouldn't be here if we thought that, would we?" said Sean.

"But goodness me, you're a very *young* news crew," said Bertha. "I've got children the same age as you. Shouldn't you all be in school?"

"We start our professional lives very early on Earth," said Nicola. "Now, do you want to be interviewed or not? Because I can always ask someone else."

"Oh, of course I would! I want to have my say! Roll the cameras! Let the universe hear how ashamed I am of my planet!"

"Be careful what you say on air, darling," said her husband.

"I've got to have my say, Bert!" said Bertha passionately.

"Okay, I want you over here." Greta took Bertha by the arm. "And I want the rest of the protesters in a sort of semi-circle behind you waving their signs."

While everyone followed Greta's instructions, Katie came over to Nicola with her beauty case. She pursed her lips professionally as she brushed blush onto Nicola's cheeks and eye shadow onto her eyelids.

"We've got to really *define* your features for television," said Katie.

"Ummm, don't forget I'm not *really* appearing on television," said Nicola quietly, as Katie agonized over the right choice of lipstick.

"Oh! Yes, of course," said Katie. It seemed like everyone was becoming caught up with their fake identities. Sean and Tyler were arguing over the best place to set up the camera equipment, while Greta was still marching around giving orders. Only Shimlara was standing still, watching the proceedings while she chewed furiously on her fingernails.

Finally, after Katie had wound Nicola's unruly hair into a bun at the back of her neck, she pronounced her ready.

"Here are your interview questions," said Greta, handing over a sheet of paper. "Use exactly the same wording I've given you. Don't say anything that isn't on the script. All you need to do is hold the microphone in front of Bertha and nod."

I'm not just your puppet, Greta, thought Nicola as she took the piece of paper.

She read the first question:

Please compare and contrast the history of the planet of Volcomania with the planet of Whimsy.

Nicola nearly choked. It sounded like an essay question. There was no way she was going to use these questions.

"Sure thing," she said to Greta.

She took a firm hold of her microphone and stood next to Bertha, who had her hands clasped in front of her and was whistling a mournful tune.

"Sorry," she said when she saw Nicola. "I always whistle sad songs when I'm nervous. It's a strange habit. You won't ask me any really *difficult* questions, will you, or try and make me look stupid?"

"Definitely not," said Nicola warmly. Knowing that Bertha was nervous filled Nicola with confidence.

"Action!" ordered Greta, in a tone of voice that made you wonder if she'd been waiting her whole life for this moment.

Nicola lifted her microphone. She had decided to use her mom's maiden name for her fake identity.

"I'm Diane Dennett, reporting live from the planet of Volcomania."

Mmmm. A bit too squeaky. Lower your voice and slow down.

"With me today, is Bertha . . ." *Frizzle! Forgot to ask her last name!* "Ah, Bertha is taking part in a protest against the War on Whimsy. Tell me, Bertha, why are you so strongly opposed to this war?"

Nicola tried not to look at Sean (he was making elaborately stupid faces at her) and held her microphone close to Bertha's mouth.

Out of the corner of her eye, she could see Greta furiously jabbing her finger at the list of questions in Nicola's hand.

"Because it's an outrage!" said Bertha.

There was an awkward pause.

"Ummm, why is it an outrage?" asked Nicola, taking the microphone back.

But she never got to hear Bertha's answer because at that moment they were both knocked off their feet by a torrent of water.

14

AS IT A FLOOD? HAD A RIVER BURST ITS banks?

Nicola went flying across the street on her stomach, propelled by an incredibly powerful surge of water. It was like she'd suddenly gone face-first down a very fast waterslide.

Gasping for breath, she sat up and looked down at her drenched clothes. Remarkably, she was still holding on to her microphone. Not one of the protesters was still standing. They were lying all over the road like flies knocked out by insecticide. Most of them had lost their placards. Some were crying.

"What happened?" she said to a young Volcomanian man lying close to her.

He sat up, dried his face on his sleeve, and pointed at the far side of the road. "Police," he said.

Nicola looked where he was pointing and saw a large group of Volcomanian women dressed in green uniforms. Each of them was holding the nozzle of an enormous black hose. The hoses looked like creepy serpent creatures.

"They turned those hoses on us?" said Nicola.

"Sure did," said the Volcomanian man grimly. "And now they'll arrest us."

"This is an *outrage!*" cried someone. Nicola looked up to see her interview subject, Bertha, climbing unsteadily to her feet and pushing her bedraggled hair out of her eyes.

"This was a legal protest against an illegal war!" she shouted.

"Oh dear," muttered the Volcomanian man.

"All protests against the war are now deemed illegal by order of Mrs. Mania!" boomed one of the policewomen. "Sit back down now, citizen!"

Bertha remained standing. "It was a peaceful protest!" she protested. "We weren't hurting anyone! We just wanted our voices to be heard!"

"*Citizen!* You must sit down now!"

"I will stand proud for my convictions," cried Bertha.

"Here we go," muttered the Volcomanian man.

WHOOOSH!

All the policewomen simultaneously turned their hoses on Bertha, hitting her directly in the stomach with a gigantic stream of water. She went flying like a rag doll and landed about a hundred feet away with a horrible wet thump.

Nicola closed her eyes. *What a cruel planet!*

"Citizens! Do not move!" boomed one of the police-women. "You will be arrested shortly and escorted to the

Protester Removal Van. Resistance of any kind will not be tolerated!"

Nobody moved.

Nicola craned her neck, looking around for the rest of the Space Brigade. Gradually she picked them all out. Everyone seemed okay, although they all looked shaken and drenched.

Would they be arrested, too? They wouldn't be much help to Shimlara's family if they were stuck in some jail.

What would a real journalist do if she found herself in this situation?

Nicola took a deep breath. A real journalist would report on the story.

She stood up.

"Are you out of your mind?" said the Volcomanian man. Nicola could see both Katie and Shimlara making frantic *"Sit down!"* gestures at her. She ignored them.

"Citizen! Are you a slow learner?" boomed the police-woman.

"I am not a citizen!" shouted Nicola, holding up her wet fake press card. "I am an Earthling journalist! My crew and I are here to report on the War on Whimsy." She pointed at her friends. "This is the Space—I mean, this is Space News from Channel, ah, Nine!" The rest of the Space Brigade stood up warily, trying hard to look dignified in their dripping tropical clothes. Together with Nicola, they picked their way through the protesters and puddles of water toward the policewomen. Nicola kept her eyes fixed on the giant hoses. She could see the policewomen were confused. They were talking nervously to one another.

She heard one policewoman say, "Let's just hose them down!"

Another one said, "But it's true Mrs. Mania doesn't like upsetting journalists from other planets."

"They're only *Earthling* journalists."

Greta spoke up. "I am the Space News producer. Obviously we only interview people in senior positions. Is there anyone qualified to appear on camera?" She gave a snooty sniff. "Or are you all . . . juniors?"

That got the policewomen bristling. Suddenly they were all arguing with one another over who should be interviewed.

"You can interview me! I'm perfectly qualified!"

"Excuse me! I'm the most senior one here."

"You! I've been in the police force since you were in diapers!"

While the policewomen were all looking at one another, the Space Brigade exchanged smiles.

"I'll interview all of you," said Nicola quickly.

"Would you all like a little lipstick first?" offered Katie.

Now the policewomen were transformed into giggly schoolgirls.

"Ooh, what colors have you got?"

"Have you got any strawberry lip gloss?"

"With my coloring, I look best with a sort of orange-brown color."

As the policewomen put down their hoses to crowd around Katie's beauty cases, Nicola noticed some of the protesters quietly getting to their feet and tiptoeing away.

She scooted around to the other side of the policewomen so that they all had to face the opposite direction from the protesters. "Who wants to be interviewed first?"

"I'm the most senior, you can interview me first," said the largest of the policewomen. She ran a fingernail around the edge of her lips and suddenly thrust her scaly-skinned face in front of Nicola with her teeth bared like a crocodile.

Nicola reeled back in horror.

"Do I have lipstick on my teeth?" asked the policewoman.

"Ah, no, they're fine." Nicola sagged with relief.

"We ready to roll?" asked Tyler, holding up the camera. Nicola hoped none of the policewomen would notice how much water was leaking out. Meanwhile Sean was squeezing water out of the sound equipment like it was a sponge.

"Action!" said Greta briskly.

Nicola spoke into her microphone. "I'm here now with a very senior member of the Volcomanian police force. These brave police have just cleverly overcome a protest against the War on Whimsy. Tell me—what will happen to these protesters now?"

"They will be all taken to the Official Prisoner of War Camp on the planet of Whimsy," answered the police-woman, darting nervous looks at the camera. "That's where all protesters against the war are being held."

There was a muffled sound from Shimlara, who was watching the filming behind Sean and Tyler.

Nicola's heart beat fast. This was her chance to find out exactly where Shimlara's family was being held.

"Ah, yes," she said. "And where exactly is that camp situated?"

"It's in Grid—" The policewoman stopped and clapped a hand over her mouth. "That's confidential information."

"Of course, of course," said Nicola smoothly. "And I believe the camp is in the southwest of Whimsy?" Of course, she had no idea where the camp was located, but she knew that people loved nothing more than correcting you when you made a mistake.

"No, it's in the *northeast*," said the policewoman in a superior tone. Then she looked furious with herself. "Stop trying to trick me into giving you top secret information! You journalists are all the same!"

"I understand," said Nicola. What else could she ask? She held out her microphone. "Are the prisoners treated well?"

"Well, it's not like they deserve five-star luxury and volcano views," snapped the policewoman. "They're *prisoners*."

"So I guess, you, ah, keep them in dark, dingy . . . caves?" hazarded Nicola.

"That would be perfect but unfortunately there are no dark, dingy caves on Whimsy," said the policewoman. "They're at the bottom of a moun—"

"What is going on here?"

A sharp voice cracked like a whip from the other side of the road.

The policewoman's red, scaly face turned a pale sort of pink color.

"It's not *her*, is it?" she whispered desperately to Nicola. "Oh, please, please tell me it's not her!"

"Quiet!"

15

NICOLA'S HAND TIGHTENED AROUND HER microphone.

On the opposite side of the Blue-5 road, a woman wearing a tailored white suit stepped gracefully out of a long, sleek black vehicle like a limousine, except with the sort of large chunky wheels you would see on a farm tractor. Even if Nicola hadn't recognized the woman from the photos the Globagaskar Chief of Special Intelligence had shown them, she would have known she was someone important. She radiated a powerful aura of authority.

"Is it *her*?" said the policewoman without turning around.

"I think it's Mrs. Mania," answered Nicola. "Your president."

"Oh *no*." The policewoman cowered as if she'd been caught doing something bad by the school principal. "Is she coming this way?"

"I think so," said Nicola sympathetically.

Mrs. Mania was striding through the puddles of water toward the policewomen and the Space Brigade. (All of the protesters, including poor Bertha, had long since crept away.) A cluster of official-looking Volcomanians in suits and dark glasses followed Mrs. Mania, scanning the crowd and making terse remarks into earpieces.

"What is going on here?" called out Mrs. Mania. "Who gave you permission to speak to the press? And where are the protesters?"

"Oh, what have I done?" moaned the policewoman. She slapped her forehead rhythmically. "I'm such a fool! I was excited to be on television! It was the *lipstick* that tempted me."

"Well, it did look lovely on you," offered Katie.

"Nicola!" hissed Tyler in Nicola's ear. "We've got to get out of here before we're recognized by the Secret Service!"

Recognized? Why would they be recognized? Suddenly Nicola remembered XYZ40 saying *the Space Brigade has quite an intergalactic reputation.*

"Well, thank you so much for your time." Nicola grabbed the policewoman's hand and shook it. "We'll be off now!"

The policewoman didn't take any notice of her. She was babbling to herself. "Fool, fool, fool!" The other members of the police force were all rubbing furiously at their lipstick with tissues and saying things like, "I *said* we shouldn't talk to the press!"

"Let's go," said Nicola quietly to the others. They all began to sidle unobtrusively toward the school bus.

"Wait!" called out Mrs. Mania. "I'd like to speak to you journalists!"

The Space Brigade froze.

Nicola didn't know what to do. If they ran, it would make them look suspicious, but if they stayed, one of the Secret Service might recognize them.

Impossible, sick-feeling-in-the-stomach decisions. That was the worst part about leading the Space Brigade. Nicola looked at Greta, who stared blankly back at Nicola as if waiting for her to decide what to do. *Mmmm*, thought Nicola crossly. *It's fine for me to be the leader when it gets hard isn't it, Greta?*

There was a sudden ruckus from Mrs. Mania's car. The back door was flung open and a figure catapulted out.

It was a girl wearing a blue dress. She spun around on the spot, clutching her neck and screaming, "Help! Someone help me!"

There was something very familiar about that voice.

"I need help this *instant*!"

"It's Princess Petronella," said Tyler.

A stout, scaly-skinned young boy had also gotten out of the back of the car and was scratching his head as he watched the princess.

"Mom!" he called to Mrs. Mania. "I think, umm—she's, ah—" He pointed hopelessly at the princess.

Mrs. Mania turned around. So did the Secret Service.

"I am choking to death!" cried Princess Petronella. "I am having an allergic reaction to the air! I am about to *die*!"

"Oh dear, is she all right?" asked Katie.

"I think she's creating a diversion for us," said Nicola. "Well, I hope that's what's she's doing. Quick! Let's go."

The Space Brigade ran toward the bus.

Shimlara threw herself down into the driver's seat, turned the key, and slammed her foot on the accelerator before anyone had a chance to sit down. They all fell around as the school bus took off, skidding across the wet road.

"Whoops!" Shimlara seized hold of the wheel and spun it back in the opposite direction. Nicola managed to pull herself into a seat just in time to see the school bus narrowly miss smashing into Mrs. Mania's limousine. She caught a quick glimpse of Princess Petronella lying flat on her back next to the limousine with the back of her hand pressed to her forehead. Nicola wasn't sure if she imagined the satisfied smirk on the princess's face.

Anyway, they were free. The bus was heading off down the Blue-5 road and it seemed everyone was so focused on the princess, they hadn't even noticed the Space Brigade leaving.

Good work, Princess Petronella.

Nicola smiled at the thought of all the praise that the princess would expect when they saw her next.

For a while, nobody said anything. They all sat in separate seats in their clammy, wet clothes, lost in their own thoughts. The only sound was the distant explosions of volcanoes. Shimlara now seemed to have the bus under control and drove it swiftly and capably. Nicola could see the Blue-5 road unfurling ahead of them like a length of ribbon. It curved to the left of the Volcomanian city ahead of them before disappearing into the fiery horizon.

Nicola pressed her hand to a sore spot on her knee where she'd fallen on the road after the policewomen had hosed them down. It gave her a strange, almost dizzy feeling thinking about it. The protesters had been trying to stand up for something they believed in but they'd been treated like criminals.

She took a deep, shaky breath.

Pull yourself together, she admonished herself.

"So let's summarize what we've learned," she said briskly.

"Will there be a quiz afterward?" said Sean, as if she was a schoolteacher.

Nicola ignored him.

She held up her hand and counted off the points on her fingers.

"We know that the prison camp is in the northeast of the planet of Whimsy. We know that its name starts with something like *Grid*. And we know that it's at the bottom of a mountain."

"We also know that the United Aunts are being held in the camp, too," said Shimlara.

"Do we?" said Nicola. "How do we know that?"

"I read Mrs. Mania's mind," said Shimlara. "As she was walking toward us, she was thinking, *If these journalists find out we're holding the United Aunts in the prison camp, the entire galaxy will turn against us.*"

"They actually kidnapped *aunties*," said Katie.

"Although I don't think these are cuddly, cookie-baking aunties," said Tyler.

"They're the most respected people in the galaxy," said Shimlara. "If we can rescue the United Aunts, we might be able to help end the War on Whimsy."

"I think we should just focus on rescuing your family, Shimlara," said Greta. "Which is going to be hard enough without trying to end the war as well. That's crazy. Anyway, why didn't you just find out where your parents were when you read Mrs. Mania's mind? That's what *I* would have done."

"When I read someone's mind, I only hear what they're thinking at that exact time," said Shimlara sharply. "I can't read every thought they've ever thought! And unfortunately

Mrs. Mania didn't happen to conveniently think about my parents."

"Oh, what's this say?" interrupted Tyler, pointing at an approaching sign. He read it out loud. "*Ten V-Miles to the Underground Sea.* That must be a Volcomanian mile, which isn't really helpful to us!"

"I can't wait to try out the scuba diving gear," said Sean.

"Me neither," said Nicola untruthfully. She tried to imagine what it would be like to breathe underwater.

"Why are you breathing funny?" said Sean, who was sitting in the seat in front of Nicola. He twisted around to look at her.

"I'm not," said Nicola.

"You sound like you've just run up thirty flights of stairs."

"Leave me alone."

Sean raised an eyebrow. He leaned forward. "You'll be fine," he said quietly. He knew that she didn't like diving underwater.

"I don't know what you're talking about," said Nicola.

Sean gave her a big brotherly smile and patted her hand.

"You'll be fine," he said again, and turned back around to face the front of the bus.

Nicola closed her eyes and tried to breathe slowly and quietly. *I'd rather parachute out of a spaceship over active volcanoes than scuba dive through that Underground Sea.*

16

WELCOME TO THE UNDERGROUND SEA: ENTRANCE TO THE PLANET OF WHIMSY

THE VOLCOMANIAN GOVERNMENT WOULD LIKE TO WARN ALL VISITORS THAT WHIMSY IS NOTORIOUS FOR ITS LACK OF PRACTICALITY AND BASIC COMMON SENSE.

WHILE SOME PEOPLE FIND THE PLANET "PRETTY AND INSPIRING," MOST SENSIBLE PEOPLE DESCRIBE IT AS "FRUSTRATING, FOOLISH, AND HOPELESSLY VAGUE." WE THEREFORE DO NOT RECOMMEND THE PLANET OF WHIMSY AS A PLEASANT TOURIST DESTINATION AND SUGGEST THAT YOU STAY IN VOLCOMANIA AND ENJOY THE CONVENIENCE AND VOLCANO VIEWS (OF WHICH THERE ARE NONE IN WHIMSY).

YOURS SINCERELY,
THE VOLCOMANIAN GOVERNMENT
SIGN NUMBER: 1049808509808508
AUTHORIZATION CODE: 494-809

THE SPACE BRIGADE WERE ALL WEARING THE scuba-diving suits provided by JJ-11 and reading a large sign on the shore of a small, ugly lake. The water was dark brown, with patches of grease floating on top, like something left over in an unwashed pot.

Everywhere they looked they could see evidence of the war being waged on Whimsy. Huge, empty buses were parked in orderly lines, each with the words, VOLCOMANIAN ARMY—WE WIN WARS! in block letters along the side. Nicola looked down and saw what looked like thousands of deep footprints in the mud, obviously left by the soldiers' boots as they marched to the lake. There were drag marks where weapons must have been pulled across the ground, and signs still standing with instructions like: LINE UP HERE FOR PROVISIONS and RESTOCK YOUR AMMUNITION HERE.

"Those must be the tanks and cannons they couldn't fit through the tunnel connecting Volcomania to Whimsy," said Sean, pointing at a number of massive gray metallic objects bobbing about in the middle of the lake.

"No wonder they couldn't fit," said Greta. Nicola followed her gaze and saw the most peculiar sight: a long, thin stone cylinder stretching out into the sky and disappearing into the horizon. It made Nicola think of those overpasses connecting shopping centers across highways. *Why does the entrance to the tunnel have to be at the bottom of a sea? It would be so much easier if you just went up an escalator!*

Shimlara picked up a pebble and threw it into the sea. "Let's hope these suits work well," she said cheerfully as the pebble vanished without a trace. "That water looks chilly!"

Volcomanian suits were very different from the rubbery suits Nicola had seen scuba divers wearing on Earth. These suits were made of fine, polished lava stone. You stepped inside and the suit automatically snapped close around your body. The insides were lined with soft fur, which felt smooth and comfortable against Nicola's skin. Instead of wearing fins on their feet, the suits had giant tails like mermaids. The tails—which doubled as storage containers for their backpacks—dragged behind them as they shuffled along, their backs bowed slightly with the weight of the heavy oxygen tanks strapped to their shoulders. They didn't have masks or snorkels like Earthling divers. Instead, their heads would be encased in large transparent bubbles of pale green glass. Right now, they were all holding the glass bubbles like footballs under their arms.

"Your hair won't even get wet," said Sean to Nicola (as if that was the only reason she was worried about scuba diving).

"Remember to watch your air supplies," said Tyler. As usual, he had been the one to read through all the instructions and learn how the suits worked. "There should be plenty of air to get us to Whimsy and back. But you have to breathe slowly and deeply, otherwise you'll use it up too quickly. If the arrow pointing at the level on your air gauge turns red, you've got five minutes to get out of the water. When it turns black—that's it, you're out of air."

Nicola imagined the panic she would feel if the arrow turned red. Just the thought of that happening made her breathe in quick, jerky gasps.

"When we get to the planet of Whimsy, don't shoot straight up to the surface," explained Tyler. "Otherwise you could get decompression sickness. You have to come up very slowly and stop for a rest every minute."

"What's decompression sickness?" asked Katie.

"It's when nitrogen bubbles form in your bloodstream," answered Tyler.

Nicola didn't like the sound of that at all.

"But if your air supply is low, you just go straight up to the top, don't you?" asked Greta.

"No, no. It's very serious. You've still got to come up slowly. That's why it's important you keep an eye on your air supply. As soon as the arrow turns red, *slowly* swim up to the surface. But that's not going to happen. The instructions say we've got enough air to get all the way to Whimsy and back."

"How are we going to see when we go through the tunnel?" said Katie. "It doesn't look like much light will get through."

Nicola suppressed a shudder (great—it would be pitch-black as well!). Tyler pushed a switch on the top of his helmet, producing a beam of strong, bright light.

"It's like a coal miner's helmet," he said with satisfaction.

"Is that it?" said Sean impatiently.

"Yes. Oh, no, one last thing, we can talk to one another underwater, which is pretty cool! Just press this Sound Transmission button." Tyler pointed to a small button on the wrist of his suit.

"Excellent. So shall we go?" said Sean eagerly, as if they were about to jump into a beautiful, crystal clear swimming pool, instead of this horrible, greasy brown lake.

"Let's go," sighed Nicola.

They shuffled their way to the edge of the lake. Everyone snapped their glass helmets over their heads and switched on their helmet lights. Nicola thought about how she'd been the first one to parachute out of the Royal Spaceship. There was no way she was going to be first this time.

Sean went striding out into the water. One minute it

was up to his knees and the next his glass helmet had vanished beneath the brown water.

Nicola gulped. *It must get deep very quickly.*

One by one, the others followed Sean. Only Nicola didn't move. She couldn't move.

She was a car without gas.

A toy with a dead battery.

"Nicola." Greta lifted her glass helmet slightly so she could speak.

Nicola didn't answer. She couldn't speak. Her vocal cords were frozen solid, like the rest of her body. The only part that was working was her brain. Her busy, terrified brain.

"Do you remember when we were on the planet of Shobble and we were learning to ride our ShobGobbles?"

Nicola did remember. Greta had been terrified. Nicola had to help her along by giving Greta's ShobGobble a quick flick of the feather-whip.

"I felt like I couldn't move," said Greta. "I was frozen with fear. That's why it was good when you got my Shob-Gobble to move. Otherwise I might have just sat there forever."

Why is she telling me all this? thought Nicola irritably. Greta wasn't normally one for taking a trip down memory lane.

"I wondered if you were feeling the same way as I did," said Greta. "So that's why I thought you might appreciate a little nudge."

She gave Nicola a firm shove in the middle of her back that sent her toppling face-first into the cold Underground Sea.

17

**ICOLA COULDN'T SEE ANYTHING EXCEPT BROWN,** murky water swirling in front of her eyes like a dust storm. She didn't know which way was up, down, left, or right.

I can't breathe! I'm drowning! It's so cold! *How dare Greta push me! I can't breathe!*

"Breathe slowly, Nicola." It was Katie's voice suddenly speaking in Nicola's ear as if they were on the phone together.

Nicola saw Katie swimming along beside her, her familiar blue eyes looking at her with concern from behind her glass bubble. She had one finger pressed to the Sound Transmission button on her wrist. Katie seemed to be moving in slow motion, like an astronaut floating through space.

Nicola's breathing slowed.

"We'll swim together," said Katie. She took hold of Nicola's hand. "No hurry. You're a good swimmer. This is just the same except you're underwater."

Nicola held on tight to Katie's hand and let her lead her to the muddy, black bottom of the Underground Sea. The others were all there, including Greta. The water wasn't quite as murky as it was near the surface, but it was still dark and shadowy, as if they'd crawled into the back of a closet. Thank goodness for the pools of light created by their helmet lights.

Although she couldn't feel the water temperature through her suit, Nicola could somehow tell it was icy cold. Long streams of tiny air bubbles floated up to the surface from near their heads. Everyone seemed to be moving in slow motion, like pieces of seaweed.

"Are you all right, Nicola?" said Sean.

"Yes," said Nicola, pressing the button on her wrist. She gave Katie's hand a quick squeeze of gratitude and let go, surprised to find that she was actually okay.

"Glad I pushed you?" asked Greta.

"I guess," said Nicola, who wasn't quite ready to forgive or thank Greta just yet. "Have you seen the tunnel entrance, Sean?"

"Yep, I'll lead the way," said Sean. "We'll have a buddy system. Katie and Nicola. Shimlara and Greta. Tyler and me. Don't lose sight of your buddy."

Everyone nodded. Sean rolled over on his stomach and held his arms close and still at his sides, so that he had a long, fishlike silhouette. He swam off with Tyler beside him. Only the tails of their suits moved, flapping slowly and rhythmically, as if the two of them had been scuba diving for years.

Shimlara and Greta followed behind them, looking just as impressive, followed by Katie and Nicola, who rolled clumsily this way and that. Nicola tried to get her tail flapping slowly like a mermaid instead of wagging like an excited puppy. She had an awful feeling she might be the only one in the Space Brigade who didn't look like a competent scuba diver. Oh well, at least she was actually swimming and not splashing around, panicking.

Sean swam toward the inky-black entrance of a tunnel about the size of a storm water drain.

As Nicola and Katie followed behind the others, the beams of light from their helmets cut through the blackness like car headlights on a deserted road.

The rocky, cavelike walls of the tunnel were covered in a black, oily substance. Slimy green weeds floated by like cobwebs. The bottom of the tunnel was covered in jagged skeleton-white shells. Not surprisingly, there wasn't a fish in sight. The word *claustrophobia* came into Nicola's head. (She loved big words with lots of syllables. They were a sort of hobby for her.)

Claustrophobia was a good word and she was pretty sure she could spell it.

It meant a fear of confined spaces.

Nicola could remember the first time she'd heard it. It was after the family had been for a visit to see their crazy great-aunt Annie, and on the way home, her dad had said that her living room made him feel claustrophobic. "She's got so many ornaments and doilies and *stuff*, I can feel the walls pressing in on me," he'd said. Nicola's mom had rolled her eyes and said, "Get a grip, Bob."

You should try this, Dad, thought Nicola. *You wouldn't be complaining about crazy Great-Aunt Annie's house then!* She tried to remember the picture she'd seen of Whimsy and Volcomania. The cylinder connecting the two planets didn't get narrower as it got closer to Whimsy, did it? That would be extremely claustrophobic.

Think about something else! Anything else! Think about—oh my goodness, look at that*!*

A school of tiny yellow fish was swimming straight toward them. It seemed like a good sign. Maybe that was a sign they were getting farther away from Volcomania and closer to Whimsy. As the fish reached the Space Brigade, they scattered and reformed, creating a funnel-like effect. It was beautiful—like silent, miniature fireworks.

"I wish I had an underwater camera," said Katie.

They continued swimming without talking. There was no sound except for the swish of their tails in the water and the sound of air bubbles.

Nicola realized that the color of the water was changing. The murky brown was gradually being replaced by a
turquoise blue. They were definitely leaving Volcomania
behind.

More schools of fish appeared. They became bigger and
brighter, with unusual shapes and intricate patterns and
colors, like tropical flowers. Nicola was enchanted.

"This is . . . *gorgeous*!"

It was Sean's voice from up ahead and it made Nicola
smile to hear him use such an un-Seanlike word as *gorgeous*.

Then she understood.

It was like she'd just entered fairyland.

Nicola reached up and switched off her helmet light.
There was no need for it anymore. Shafts of gold light from
somewhere up ahead were bathing the tunnel in a gauzy
stream. The slimy weeds and jagged shells and frightfully
strange-looking fish had disappeared. Instead, they were
swimming through a kaleidoscope of colorful coral. Lavish
ruby-red petals and gold feathers swayed as if in a breeze.
There were explosions of emerald green and boulders of sapphire blue. Nicola's eyes feasted as if on a glorious banquet.

The farther they swam, the more beautiful and bizarre
the sea life became, appearing and disappearing, as if she
were watching an illuminated merry-go-round.

A sea horse swam by with kind eyes on long stalks and

floating baubles like the fringe of a shawl. A furry-skinned tortoise scurried along the sand. A creature with a comical, monkeylike face poked its head out from behind a piece of coral and then quickly pulled it back again.

And swimming right along beside her, as if it were keeping her company, was a long, sleek, white . . . shark.

Nicola swiveled her eyes to look at it.

It had the tiny, mean eyes of a rat and the snarling mouth of an alligator.

Of course, just because it looked like a nasty piece of work didn't mean it was dangerous. After all, sharks on the planet of Whimsy might be whimsical, arty creatures. They might be *pets*!

Then again, this shark had come from behind her. So it was probably more likely it was from Volcomania than Whimsy.

She realized she should stop calling it a shark. That was an Earthling word. It might be called something quite different here. She wouldn't feel as frightened about it if it were called, for example, a teddy bear. *Oh, look at the nice teddy bear*, she would think to herself.

Although, even if it were called a teddy bear, she still wouldn't like the look of those sharp, pointy teeth.

"Nicola," said Katie. "Don't look now, but there is a horrible shark swimming right next to you."

"It's not a shark," said Nicola. "It's a teddy bear."

"Huh?" said Katie.

Whatever the creature was called, it suddenly swam ahead, moving straight and fast like an expertly thrown dart.

"Shimlara! Greta! Watch out behind you!" called Nicola.

The shark stopped.

"Oh no," said Katie quietly.

It swam back around to face them, as if it were squaring up for a fight.

Now Nicola saw that it didn't look that much like an Earthling shark at all. It had a curved horn in the middle of its forehead. A horn like you might see on a rhinoceros.

It didn't make it look any friendlier or more teddylike. In fact—

"Watch out!" screamed Katie.

The shark-rhino was swimming straight for Nicola.

Katie grabbed Nicola's arm and dragged her out of the way. Nicola heard the creature's horn clink against the glass of the bubble protecting her face.

"It's coming after you!" cried Shimlara. "Swim!"

Nicola and Katie swam as if they'd just heard the starter gun for the most important race of their lives.

Greta and Shimlara took off, too. The frantic flapping of their mermaid tails created a washing-machine effect.

As Nicola tried to see through the whirlpool of frothy white water, her eye was caught by something.

The little arrow on the inside of her scuba diving suit's glass bubble had turned red. She had less than five minutes before her air ran out.

18

HICH WOULD I PREFER? THOUGHT NICOLA.

Option A: a vicious underwater attack by a shark-rhino?

Option B: running out of air in the claustrophobic Underground Sea?

Option C: painful, possibly fatal, decompression sickness from swimming too fast to the surface?

NONE OF THE ABOVE, screamed Nicola silently.

She looked up and saw she couldn't swim to the surface even if she wanted. She would just bump her head on the top of the tunnel and the shark-rhino would have her cornered. She knew that she should have been breathing slowly and calmly to conserve the last precious drops of oxygen but it was impossible. She was breathing in giant, panicky gulps.

"Nicola!" cried Katie. She pointed at Nicola's leg. "It's got you!"

Nicola turned her head and was aghast to see that the shark-rhino had its huge mouth clamped around her leg.

Pain! Blood! Impending death!

But actually . . . interestingly . . . she couldn't feel a thing.

She could see the shark-rhino was doing its very best to take a large, satisfying bite out of her leg, but it was like it was trying to munch a leathery piece of steak. As Nicola watched, one of its sharp, pointy teeth actually snapped off and floated away. The shark-rhino pulled away from Nicola's leg with an offended look and swam off in a huff.

Nicola laughed out loud with relief. "Our scuba diving suits are made of lava stone!" she called out to Katie. "They're impossible to break! We're perfectly safe!"

Then she heard a shout from ahead.

It was Sean's voice.

"We're here! This is Whimsy!"

Nicola and Katie swam in the direction of his voice.

The tunnel came to an abrupt end and they swam out into a vastly different world.

Directly below Nicola was an endless landscape of colorful coral, like a mountaintop of wildflowers. Everywhere she looked, she could see schools of brilliantly colored fish and more weird and wonderful sea creatures, some tiny and exquisite, others huge and magnificent. When she looked up, she could see the transparent, rippled surface of the water swishing back and forth like a bedsheet fluttering in the breeze on a clothesline, and far, far above that, a blue sky.

Nicola didn't want to go up to the surface. It was too

beautiful down here. She could stay forever! She loved the weightless feeling of scuba diving. It was all so incredibly beautiful, she wanted to write a poem about it. How could it begin?

Like a bird, I skim and fly
Through prisms of sun-dappled sapphire
Like a ...

"Remember to ascend slowly!" Tyler's voice broke through her thoughts like a slap across her face.

Nicola saw the red arrow on the air gauge directly in front of her eyes and remembered that she was nearly out of air.

What a fool! She could have wasted the remaining air she had left writing poetry! She really would have to be careful not to let this planet's beauty make her forget to concentrate.

"Okay, let's go up!" she said to the others.

"I think I'll stay down here for another hour or so," said Katie dreamily. "I've got an idea for a symphony! It goes like this. La-da-da-dum, la-da-da-da-da-dum!"

Nicola saw Katie's eyes had a dazed, unfocused look. She remembered how XYZ40 had warned them that she and Katie might be more susceptible to Whimsy's beauty than the others.

"Katie!" said Nicola sharply. "You can't stay down here

composing symphonies! We've got to rescue Shimlara's family!"

"Oh!" Katie blinked and her eyes came into focus. "Of course we do! Sorry!"

Slowly and carefully, stopping for breaks, the Space Brigade swam up to the surface.

Nicola kept a careful eye on her air gauge. Her breathing had slowed right down. She had never realized that beauty could have an actual physical effect.

Just as the arrow turned black, Nicola's head broke through the surface of the water.

She was first up. She pulled the glass bubble off her head and treaded water as she breathed in air so pure and sweet, she felt like she was drinking it.

Oh my goodness, this is . . .

The rest of the Space Brigade emerged from the water around her.

She smiled as she saw the expressions of amazement and delight on their faces as they gazed around them.

"Welcome to the planet of Whimsy," she said.

19

HE SPACE BRIGADE PULLED OFF THEIR HELMETS and took a look at their surroundings. All of them were struggling to find the right words to describe Whimsy.

"Oh, it's just . . . !" said Katie.

"This is . . . this is . . . this is . . . ," repeated Sean over and over.

"I have never seen anything so . . . so . . . I don't know," said Shimlara.

"Beautiful," said Greta. "Except beautiful seems too ordinary a word. It's . . ."

"Ineffable," said Nicola.

They all stared at her as if she were speaking another language.

"It's a word!" Nicola said defiantly. "I saw it in the dictionary one day when I was looking up how to spell inertia. *Ineffable* means something that you can't describe. I didn't think I'd ever get to use that word, but that's what this is— ineffable."

She gestured at their surroundings. They were in the very center of a brilliant turquoise lake. Waterfalls tumbled over mossy rocks. Birds soared above them, singing like church bells. In the distance, they could see velvet green mountains. The sky was the color of a ripe plum. There was only one sun, just like on Earth, except this sun was four times the size of Earth's sun, and it shone beams of intense scarlet-gold light. Curving over the sky like a rainbow, and hiding Volcomania's suns and volcanoes from view, was the halo of pink atmospheric dust. From here, you would never know that Whimsy was attached to a planet like Volcomania.

BOOM! BOOM! BOOM!

A shocking sound ripped through the peaceful landscape. One of the velvet-green mountains exploded inward as if a giant fist had punched it. Clouds of smoke billowed black against the plum-colored sky. There was a hammering noise that sounded like machine guns.

The Space Brigade swam closer together and formed a tight little circle of fear. The joy on their faces vanished. They'd forgotten they were in a war zone.

"Let's get to the shore," said Nicola.

As they swam, more explosions rocked the lake like an earthquake. Suddenly Nicola was furious with Volcomania. What right did it have to declare war on this beautiful planet? It was like a big bully picking on an adorable child.

"Leave them *alone*!" she cried at the sky.

Fortunately, it didn't take them long to make it to the

sandy shore. They unsnapped their scuba-diving suits and stepped out, their clothes completely dry.

"Maybe we should hide our suits here instead of carrying them around everywhere we go," said Katie.

"Good idea," said Nicola.

They found a cave behind a waterfall and hid their suits under a pile of rocks.

"I hope we get to use these," said Shimlara, her voice filled with emotion, as she hid the three extra suits they'd brought along for Georgio, Mully, and Squid.

"Of course we'll use them," said Nicola.

"Mmmm—" began Greta with a pessimistic look on her face but Nicola glared at her, making a sign with her finger and thumb like a zipper pulling her mouth shut. For once Greta stopped talking.

"We have to remember we're still undercover as a news crew," said Nicola. "So don't forget your press passes."

"No problem," said Tyler. "As long as no one looks too closely at our equipment." He lifted his battered and soggy camera gear onto his shoulder.

"What will I be now that I'm not the bus driver?" said Shimlara.

"You can be my assistant," said Greta. "That means you get me cups of coffee and schedule my meetings and stuff like that."

Shimlara raised her eyebrows. "Seeing as I've never even heard of coffee, and I don't know how to 'schedule a meeting,' I don't think I'd make much of an assistant."

"You can be our bodyguard," said Nicola. "It makes sense seeing as you're so much taller than us."

Shimlara liked that idea immediately. She lifted her fists like a fighter and spoke in a deep, weirdly accented voice. "You wanna take me on? Do ya? Well, do ya?"

She chuckled as if she'd just said something that they would all agree was hilarious. Then she saw the rest of the Space Brigade staring at her blankly. "You know! It's a line from that movie *Galaxy Bust*! You know, the part where the bad guy is talking to himself in the mirror? You must have seen it. I've seen it fourteen times. Every single person I *know* has seen *Galaxy Bust*!"

"We don't get to see movies from other planets on Earth," explained Nicola.

Shimlara dropped her fists. "Well, anyway, I'll be your security guard, no problem. You're all under my protection. No one gets hurt on my watch."

"I don't need you to protect me," said Sean.

"It's just a *role*, Sean," said Nicola. "It's not real. Remember?"

"Yeah, I know that," muttered Sean. "I'm just saying . . ."

Shimlara winked at Nicola over Sean's head.

"I *saw* that!" said Sean.

KABOOM!

There was another explosion from outside the cave. It was even louder than the ones they'd heard before.

"I think I miss the volcanoes," said Katie.

"Shhhh." Tyler held up his hand. "Did you hear that?"

"The explosion?" said Sean. "A bit hard to miss."

"No," said Tyler. "It sounded like someone calling for help."

"I can't hear anything," said Greta. "You're imagining it."

"I am not imagining it," said Tyler. Nicola had never seen him speak so assertively. "Be quiet, all of you, and listen!"

Everyone stopped talking. There was silence. The bombs had stopped and they could hear the birds singing again.

Nicola went to speak and then she heard it. They all heard it.

It was someone screaming. A woman's voice, raw with panic.

"Help! Please!"

The Space Brigade ran.

20

**YLER TOOK THE LEAD.**

"This way!" he called, running out of the cave and around the shore of the lake.

The voice rang out again. "Is anyone there? I need help!"

"We're coming!" called Tyler.

They scrambled over mossy rocks and ran along a wooden bridge that crossed a bubbling creek. Suddenly they were in a forest. Trees with creamy, papery bark and giant red leaves towered above them, and Nicola caught a glimpse of small, big-eyed animals scurrying through the branches.

Tyler came to an abrupt stop. "I don't know which way to go," he said.

They all stopped, breathing heavily and trying to listen for the voice. They had come to a small clearing. Numerous trails ran off the clearing in different directions. "I think I can hear children," said Katie, her face creased with worry.

Nicola could hear shouts and cries in the distance but she had no idea which direction they were coming from.

"Smoke!" said Shimlara suddenly. "This way!" She took off down one of the trails. They ran behind her.

Now Nicola could hear the distressed cries of very young children.

"I want my mommy!"

"I can't see!"

"I hurt myself!"

The Space Brigade picked up their pace.

The trail ended in a small hollow.

"Oh, thank goodness you're here!" A young woman with a long, blond braid down her back came running out of the smoke toward them. She was clutching a wilting yellow flower and wearing a rose-colored dress with puffy sleeves and a big sash tied in a bow at the back. Even though her face was stained with tears and soot, and there was a bloody gash down one cheek, you could see she was very beautiful.

"They've attacked my preschool with a bubble-bomb!" she cried. "There are twenty children in there! Twenty of the most *adorable* small children! We were reading stories when little Camille noticed this yellow buttercup through the window. Well, she loves flowers! They all do! So naturally, I ran straight out to pick it for her and when I turned around—*kaboom*! Bubbles were everywhere! It was impossible to see a thing! It was so frightening! How could this happen?"

She clung to Tyler's arm.

"I—don't know," stammered Tyler. He seemed overcome by the woman's beauty and the strange scene in front of them.

Through the haze of smoke, Nicola could see an enormous mass of quivering, frothy white soap bubbles. It was like a giant bubble bath or a washing machine had overflowed.

"My preschool is under all those bubbles!" babbled the woman. "We have to get the children out before those awful soldiers arrive! That's what the Volcomanian Army does! They drop a bubble-bomb from the air, and while everyone is trapped—confused, blinded, and *sticky*!—they send the soldiers in to capture them! It's pure evil!"

Without even looking at one another, as if they were responding to some unheard order, every member of the Space Brigade ran straight into the mass of bubbles.

Nicola was immediately disoriented. All she could see was white froth. It was like being trapped in the middle of a cloud.

"Where are you, kids?" she shouted, batting helplessly away at the bubbles. Her eyes were stinging, and her mouth was filled with the taste of soap.

"We're all still sitting on the story mat!"

"We can't see anything!"

Nicola turned toward the voices and slipped, painfully banging her knee against something.

"I think the entrance is this way!" Nicola heard Sean's voice in front of her.

Nicola got back up to her feet and followed his voice, up what seemed to be a small step and in through a doorway.

"My clothes are all *bubbly*!" The voice seemed to come from somewhere near Nicola's feet. She got down on her hands and knees and crawled slowly forward, calling out, "Where are you?" Suddenly her hand clutched a small foot.

"That tickles!"

Nicola pushed away the bubbles to reveal a cheekily grinning little girl scooping bubbles out of her hair. "This is a fun game!" she said. "Is it like hide-and-seek?"

"Sort of." Nicola stood up. "Come with me and I'll take you to your teacher."

The little girl stood up and grabbed her hand. Slipping and sliding, blindly trying to find her way back to the front door, Nicola managed to drag her out of the mass of bubbles and back into the clearing.

She turned to see the rest of the Space Brigade emerging from the school. Sean had a child sitting happily astride his shoulders, while Shimlara, being the tallest, had managed to scoop up two at once. Apart from being covered in bubbles, so they all looked like miniature snowmen, the children seemed perfectly happy.

"Oh! Oh! My darlings! My sweeties!" The preschool teacher tried to hug them all at once.

There were still voices coming from inside the preschool, so Nicola and the others brushed the bubbles from their eyes and ran straight back in to pull out more children.

This time Nicola found a little boy humming happily to himself in the corner.

"I'm staying here," he told Nicola. "These bubbles are *beautiful*!"

"No, you're not," said Nicola firmly, grabbing him by the elbow and pulling him outside.

"How many are still in there?" asked Greta, grunting with relief as she deposited a rather plump child at the teacher's feet.

The teacher looked confused.

"Oh, I'm not sure. Let me see, we're still missing dear little Sebastian, aren't we? Oh, no we're not—here he is! Yes, Sebastian, I'm sure we'll find your violin. Have you glorious people come across Sebastian's violin by any chance?"

"That's not important right now!" Greta was exasperated. "We need to know how many more children we need to save!"

"Yes, yes, of course you do," said the teacher. "Children are far more important than violins! It's just that I can't seem to count the children! They're like marbles, rolling this way and that."

Greta sighed and wiped a layer of bubbly froth from her face. "Right!" she cried like an army officer. "All children line up in front of me *now*!" The children jumped and immediately ran to obey her orders.

Greta counted them efficiently. "Sixteen, seventeen, eighteen, nineteen. *Nineteen!* So that means we're still missing one child, right?"

"Yes," said the teacher. "I definitely have twenty children in my class because that's how many strawberry frosted cupcakes I make on strawberry frosted cupcake day!"

The Space Brigade renewed their efforts—running back into the preschool, slipping and sliding, tearing their fingernails, and grazing their knees as they searched through the bubbles for the last missing child.

After ten minutes, just when Nicola was beginning to feel quite frantic, the teacher suddenly cried, "Oh, I forgot Jerry Sweet!" The Space Brigade went back outside.

"Jerry Sweet!" said the teacher happily. "I always make him an extra strawberry frosted cupcake because he loves them so much, so I let you have two, don't I, Jerry?"

The fat-cheeked little boy whom Greta had saved nodded and licked his lips solemnly.

"So that means I must have nineteen children in my class, not twenty!" said the teacher. "Goodness, what a lot of complex mathematics I'm doing today!"

"So we've definitely got everyone?" double-checked Nicola.

"Yes," said the teacher. "Yes, you do! You're heroes!"

"What's that?" Tyler lifted his head. Nicola couldn't hear a thing. Tyler seemed to have developed superhuman hearing.

And then she heard a pounding of footsteps coming their way like a great herd of elephants.

"Is it Volcomanian soldiers already?" asked Sean.

The teacher looked terrified. "Oh, quick, quick, we must hide, get back under the bubbles, darlings!"

At that moment, a crowd of people poured into the clearing and the teacher's face broke into a smile.

"It's not soldiers!" she said happily. "It's the parents!"

21

HE PARENTS WERE HALF-CRAZED WITH FEAR. They stumbled and tripped and shouted. When they saw their children, they grabbed them in suffocating embraces and repeated their names over and over.

"We expected the worst when we heard the preschool had been hit," said one of the mothers to the teacher. "But you managed to save them all, you clever girl, Rosie!"

"No, no!" said Rosie. "It wasn't me, it was these wonderful apparitions! It was like magic. I called for help, and they appeared with a puff of smoke and a sprinkle of stardust! They set to work, rescuing the children with the use of their superpowers! Look at them, aren't they lovely! Someone must paint their portraits and sculpt their statues!"

The Space Brigade squirmed with embarrassment as the parents dropped their children and ran to hug them.

"We are forever in your debt!"

"How shall we ever repay you?"

"Shouldn't we get out of here?" asked Tyler. "Won't the Volcomanian soldiers be here soon?"

"See how *intelligent* they are!" beamed Rosie.

"We shall take you to our village and give you a feast in your honor!" cried the parents.

"Oh, that's really not nec—" began Nicola, but the children had already grabbed them with their sticky hands and were dragging them away from the bubble-covered pre-school and down a pathway that led out of the forest.

"What magical planet are you from?" asked one of the parents.

Nicola decided it would be best if they stayed under-cover. Although these people were clearly not Volcoma-nians, she had learned from her experiences on the planet of Shobble that you could never be too careful.

"We're journalists from Earth," she said. "We're reporting on the war. We don't have any magical powers at all and we're definitely not superheroes—we were just happy to help."

The parents refused to believe that magic wasn't involved in some way.

"It was magic that put you in the right place at the right time," they agreed.

"Just good luck," said Sean.

"Exactly," said one of the fathers with dark hair, a pale face, and soulful eyes. "Luck. Magic. Same thing. I once tried to write a poem on exactly that topic. It didn't really come together. I must try again." He wandered off, pulling a small notepad from his pocket and a pencil from behind his ear.

One of the mothers was looking at Shimlara. "You're not from the planet Earth, are you, my dear? You're far too tall. Actually, there's something familiar about your lovely young face."

"I'm from Globagaskar," said Shimlara.

"Ah." The mother frowned. Then her face cleared. "You must be Georgio and Mully Gorgioskio's daughter! You're an exact mix of the two of them. Georgio's nose. Mully's mouth." The woman looked around excitedly. "Are your delightful parents here, too?"

"Ah, no, they're not," said Shimlara. "Well, we think they could be here on Whimsy, but, um—"

She glanced at Nicola, obviously not sure how much she should say.

"How do you know Georgio and Mully?" Nicola asked the mother.

"They visited Whimsy the day after Volcomania declared war on us," said the woman. "They were so charming! They gave us a list of things we should do to try and prevent the war. You see, my husband is Henry Sweet—he's the new president of Whimsy, although it does keep slipping his mind. Where is Henry?"

"Right behind you, my love!" A man wearing a beret,

with spatters of paint across his face, was walking behind them, carrying the little plump boy who liked cupcakes on his hip. Nicola recognized the man from the pictures that XYZ40 had shown them at the intelligence briefing.

"This is Georgio and Mully's daughter," said the woman.

Henry nearly dropped his son as he bowed deeply.

"There are no words that can express my gratitude for the gift of my son's life. It plunges deeper than the ocean, it soars higher than an eagle."

"Ah, that's okay," said Shimlara. "Um, your wife was saying that my parents were here?"

"Indeed they were. They could only stay for a day. They had to get back to Globagaskar. They said they had a small son who was being babysat by his grandma and a daughter who was away on the planet of Shobble." He looked at Shimlara and Nicola, and said, "Well, you must be the Space Brigade!"

Their cover was blown.

"Georgio told us the whole story of how the Space Brigade was formed. He's very proud of you." He looked confused. "So you're also journalists? As well as undertaking daring missions around the galaxy? Goodness, you're busy."

Nicola decided she might as well be honest. "We're not really journalists. That's just our cover story for the Volcomanians. We're really here to try and find Georgio, Mully, and their little boy, Squid. After they returned to Globagas-kar, we believe they were kidnapped by the Volcomanian government and brought back here to Whimsy. We think they're being held in a prison camp."

Henry's face went pale beneath the splatters of paint.

"They were imprisoned for trying to help us," he said. "That's terrible."

"Yes," said his wife. Her face crumpled. "And to think that you *lost* their list of suggestions for preventing the war!"

"I did! I thought I put it in my pocket and it disap-peared!" Henry gave an anguished cry. "And now their daughter has saved our son!"

"Well, actually, I think it was *me* that pulled out your kid," pointed out Greta.

Henry wasn't listening. He had curled his hand into a fist and was beating it against his chest. "Those poor, kind people! Imprisoned for helping us!"

It's true, thought Nicola, *the people of Whimsy are quite incredibly impractical.*

The children were now leading them to the edge of the forest. Nicola could see the shore of the lake and thatched rooftops in the distance. Their village must be close.

"Well," she said. "Maybe you could help us *find* the prison camp where Georgio and Mully are being held. It's in the northeast of your planet at the bottom of a mountain and it has a name beginning with something like *Grid*."

"That would be Griddlemill," said Henry's wife. "The Volcomanians have a prison camp there? But that's terrible! That's where Henry proposed to me! They have the most beautiful roses you have ever seen in Griddlemill. The scent is so exquisite, I once composed an opera about it. Let me sing a little for you." She threw back her head and a sound like a nightingale burst forth. "Tra la la la!"

She stopped singing abruptly. "And if you suffer from insomnia, simply crush a few Griddlemill rose petals into your tea and you'll sleep past noon. Lovely taste, too!"

"I'll remember that." Nicola tried not to let her impatience show. The children had now led them out of the forest, through the archway of a moss-covered wall, and onto a cobblestone street. "But perhaps you could take us there? Or at least give us directions? To Griddlemill?"

"Of course," said Henry. "But first we must feast!" He lifted his arms flamboyantly. "For we are home! Welcome to our village, Space Brigade!"

22

THE SPACE BRIGADE SAT AT THE HEAD OF A LONG, beautifully carved wooden table covered with flowers, in the center of the village square.

The village was built right on the side of the lake, so that everywhere they looked they could see the dancing reflections of the water. The cottages had cherry-red front doors, fluttering lace curtains, and window boxes overflowing with flowers.

After endless discussion (much of it pointless and involving reciting of poetry and singing of songs), it had finally been agreed that after the feast in their honor, he, President Henry Sweet, would lead the Space Brigade to Griddlemill at Diamond-Moon. Apparently that was when Whimsy's four moons formed a diamond shape in the night sky.

"The Volcomanian army always goes to bed straight after Diamond-Moon," Henry Sweet had explained. "They're running this war according to a strict schedule. Now you're probably wondering about the word *schedule*. I'd never heard of it, either. You see, Volcomanians *plan* what they're going to do at certain times each day and then they *stick to the plan*. Can you imagine anything more horrible or restrictive? It reminds me of too-tight pants."

"We have schedules and timetables on Earth," said Greta. "They're actually very useful."

"Oh," said Henry, with a horrified expression as if Greta had just admitted that the Earthlings never bathed. "I do beg your pardon."

"I guess you could say that if we're leaving at Diamond-Moon, then we're planning ahead, so we've got a schedule ourselves," pointed out Tyler.

That was too much for Henry. He mumbled something about feeling dizzy, and vanished.

"I can't believe he's the president of this planet," hissed Greta. "He's a fruitcake."

"They're artists," said Katie.

She pointed at the Whimsians of the village. Some of them were sculpting statues of the Space Brigade. Many of them had easels set up and were painting their portraits. Another group was rehearsing a musical all about the "day the children were saved." They could just make out some of the lyrics:

"And just when all hope was lost,

And we thought we would pay a most terrible cost!

The Space Brigade turned up like sun after rain . . .
after raiiiiin . . . after raiiiiiiiin!"

"I know they're artists but that's no excuse for being so hopeless," said Greta.

"You sound like a Volcomanian," said Shimlara. "Next thing you'll be saying this war is justified."

"War is terrible," said Greta. "But I can sort of understand why Volcomania finds Whimsy so, well, frustrating."

"I wonder if this feast will actually include food," said Sean worriedly. "Remember how XYZ40 said they forget to eat? And I guess Volcomania has cut off their food supply."

"There are more important things to worry about than food," said Nicola, although she was actually feeling very hungry herself. They hadn't eaten since their breakfast that morning in Volcomania.

"I think we're going to be okay," said Tyler. "Look!"

Whimsians were appearing from every direction, staggering under the weight of gigantic platters containing the most extraordinarily beautiful desserts.

There were towering cakes of shaved chocolate and whipped cream.

There were meringues piled high with sugar-speckled strawberries.

There were flaky pastries adorned with lacy toffee sculptures.

"They look too good to eat," commented Katie. "Each one is a work of art!"

"I think I'll still manage to eat them," said Sean.

The Whimsians placed the desserts on the long table and then stood back with their hands clasped in front of them, their heads bowed demurely, as if waiting for applause.

"Ummm," said Nicola uncertainly. She looked at the others. There was no silverware or plates. Were they meant to eat with their hands? Maybe that was the custom on the planet of Whimsy? She didn't want to offend anyone by asking for spoons if they didn't exist. On the other hand, it seemed very rude (and messy) to just dig in to these beautiful desserts.

While Nicola was still trying to figure out what to do, Shimlara spoke up.

"These look absolutely wonderful," she said politely. "But we're just not sure how you eat them?"

The Whimsians looked perplexed and then they slapped their foreheads and cried, "Silverware! Why do we always forget silverware?"

All the Whimsians blushed in unison, their faces flushing a rather lovely crimson color. Some of them wept. Others sat down, their heads in their hands.

"We are so *foolish*!"

"We're hopeless!"

"The feast is ruined!"

"There's really no problem," said Sean. "Could you maybe, ah, grab us the silverware?"

"Oh!" they cried, as if they hadn't even thought of there being an actual solution to the problem. "Of course!" They ran off, back to their cottages.

"For heaven's sake," said Greta.

"I'd take small bites of these desserts," whispered Shimlara. "They seem like the sort of cooks who might accidentally use salt instead of sugar."

The Whimsians ran off and returned with piles of plates, knives, and spoons. The Space Brigade served themselves and took tentative bites.

"Ahhhhhhh," they all said at once. The desserts tasted as exquisitely beautiful as they looked. The Whimsians beamed with pleasure and an orchestra struck up a celebratory tune.

"Is Volcomania still supplying your food now that they're at war with you?" said Nicola to Henry Sweet's wife.

"No, they've cut us right off!" said Mrs. Sweet, as if this was a rather fascinating development. "We used the very last scraps of our food to make these desserts."

"Oh no." Nicola put down her spoon. "You shouldn't have! What will you do now?"

"About what?" said Mrs. Sweet sweetly.

"About food?"

"Oh, I'm not at all hungry, thank you. I had an enormous piece of the chocolate meringue."

"Yes, but you will be hungry later, and you'll have nothing to eat."

Mrs. Sweet smiled politely, as if she had absolutely no idea what Nicola was talking about. The concept of planning ahead was obviously completely foreign to her. "Do excuse me," she said. "I just thought of a rather interesting plot twist for my novel."

An hour later, Sean was the only one in the Space Brigade still eating. The rest of them had finally laid down their spoons and joined the Whimsians, who were lying around on picnic blankets watching the stars appear in the evening sky.

It was like watching fine pieces of jewelry laid out on a midnight blue satin cloth. Each star was a different color and shape. There was a soft green oval like an antique brooch, a string of tiny teardrops like a diamond bracelet.

Nicola licked leftover sugar from her fingers and was surprised to find her eyes filling with tears.

"Your planet is so beautiful it hurts my heart," she said to Rosie, the preschool teacher, who was lying next to her.

"I know what you mean," sighed Rosie, pulling her long braid over her shoulder. "Every day when the sun rises, tears of joy stream down my face."

"That's all very well," said Greta, who was sitting up cross-legged on the blanket next to Rosie and Nicola and not even bothering to look at the stars. "But you do realize your planet is at war right now? And you're all just lying around admiring the sky? Your school was *bombed* today!"

"Greta," sighed Nicola. She thought that Greta was being extremely rude. "Oh! Look at this star! It's like a giant ruby!"

"Shouldn't some of you be guarding the perimeter of your village? Or working out your defense strategies?" continued Greta. "Do you have any strategies at all? You're going to lose this war!"

"I'm sure you're right," said Rosie vaguely. "We have no experience with war. We don't really like war, to be frank."

"Nobody likes war!" said Greta. "But you've still got to fight back!"

"Mmmm," said Rosie. "Do you think we could talk of something more pleasant? That particular topic is making my head ache."

Greta groaned with frustration.

Nicola closed her eyes so she could no longer see the stars. The sensible part of her mind knew that Greta had a point. It would be terrible if the planet of Whimsy were to lose the war and their independence. It was just so hard to even think about it when everything was so distractingly beautiful.

Anyway, what could they do about it? They weren't here to help Whimsy win the war. They were here to rescue Shimlara's family and that was enough of a challenge.

"Is that the Diamond-Moon?" said Sean from the feast table. It sounded like his mouth was still stuffed full of cake.

Nicola opened her eyes and saw that four silvery moons had appeared in the sky in the shape of a diamond.

She stood up and shook her head vigorously, trying to clear the fuzzy feeling created by all that starlight and sugar. She felt like she needed to eat a straightforward ham sandwich on brown bread and work on a difficult math problem.

"Where is Henry Sweet?" she said, trying to make her voice firm and decisive, rather than soft and dreamy. "It's time we left for Griddlemill."

23

T WAS ANOTHER HOUR BEFORE THEY FINALLY SET
off. Nobody had been able to find Henry Sweet. He'd
finally been discovered in the studio of his cottage
painting a giant canvas bright orange.

"I have an idea for a new painting," he said, with
a feverish light in his eyes.

"That's wonderful, darling!" said his wife. "Well, in
that case, we must leave you to it." She turned to the
Space Brigade. "Perhaps we could postpone your journey
until tomorrow night? Or next week? When the artistic
mood strikes, Henry does nothing but paint. I'm sure you'll
understand."

But all that time they'd spent looking for Henry had
well and truly cured Nicola of her beauty overload and put
her in a cranky mood. She was also feeling queasy from
eating too much dessert.

"That's not possible," she said. "We must get to Griddlemill as soon as possible. Don't forget that the Gorgioskios
are only in the prison camp because they cared so much
about your planet. And by the way, I don't mean to be rude,
but you're the *president* and your planet is under attack!

You should be thinking of your people, not your next painting!"

Henry dropped his paintbrush with a splatter of orange paint.

"You're right! Of course, you're right! I'd forgotten I was president! And I'd forgotten we were at war!" He collapsed on to a small stool and looked anguished. "And you saved my child today! I'm a terrible, terrible, person. My selfishness is like a snake wrapped around my heart, it's like a—oh!"

Sean and Shimlara had grabbed him by the elbows and hauled him to his feet.

"We don't have time for this, buddy," said Sean kindly. "You've got to pull yourself together."

Henry took a deep breath and straightened his beret. "You're right," he said. "Follow me."

"What sort of transportation will we be taking?" asked Tyler.

"Transportation?" said Henry with a furrowed brow.

"I think we're walking," said Nicola to Tyler.

"How long will that take us?" frowned Shimlara.

"We shall *run*!" cried Henry passionately.

"Oh, well, that's not really nec—" began Nicola.

But Henry had already run off, his paint-splattered smock billowing behind him.

"Goodbye, my brave darling!" cried his wife, her hands clasped together. Then she said under her breath, "This will make such a wonderful scene in my novel. *His smock billowed like the sail of a boat . . .* No, that's not quite right."

The Space Brigade had no choice but to run after Henry, their backpacks bouncing against their shoulders, the desserts they'd eaten sitting heavily in their stomachs.

Henry ran straight up a hill. His skinny legs leaped nimbly over hedges as he carefully avoided crushing flowers.

"He's very fit for an artist," panted Katie.

"I think I'm going to be sick," moaned Sean. His face was green in the starlight. "I might have overdone it on the desserts."

"Are we going to run the whole way there?" groaned Greta.

"They must have *some* sort of transport on this planet," wheezed Tyler.

"What's wrong with running?" Shimlara jogged effortlessly up the hill on her long legs.

Nicola couldn't speak. She was too busy trying to breathe. Long-distance running wasn't her thing.

After what seemed like at least an hour of solid running, Henry suddenly stopped.

He was down on his hands and knees on the shore of a

river, scooping up water to drink with cupped hands, when the Space Brigade caught up with him.

"Isn't this exhilarating?" cried Henry when he saw them arrive.

The Space Brigade fell to their knees, breathing heavily. Sean dipped his face in the water and lapped it up like an exhausted dog. As Nicola drank the cool, refreshing water, she could feel beads of sweat running down her back. Her tired legs felt like jelly. She didn't know how much longer she could keep running.

"Now we just follow the river," said Henry. "All the way to Griddlemill."

"How long should that take?" asked Shimlara.

"No more than a few weeks," said Henry cheerfully. "If we run all the way. And if we avoid Volcomanian bubble-bombs."

There was silence as the Space Brigade digested this distressing new information.

"I don't want to leave my family in a prison camp for that long!" said Shimlara.

"Is there no quicker way to get there?" asked Nicola desperately. The thought of running like that every day was enough to make her long to be back on Earth, sitting comfortably in the passenger seat of her mother's car, watching joggers run by.

"But how else could we get there?" asked Henry. "If only we were birds, we could flap our wings and soar, but alas, we are not!"

"What if we had a canoe?" said Tyler. "We could just canoe straight down the river."

"Canoe?" said Henry, in a way that showed the word was unfamiliar to him.

"They obviously don't have canoes on this planet," said Greta.

Tyler looked around him for inspiration.

He ran to a nearby tree and snapped off a branch. "We could make a raft!"

"Roft?" said Henry. "What is a roft?"

"Could we make one that wouldn't sink?" asked Sean. "And how would we bind the branches together?"

"With this," said Greta, and she bent down and picked up a length of green curly vine from the shore of the river. She tugged on both ends to demonstrate its strength. "Perfect."

"But we don't know *how* to make a raft," said Katie. "Do we?"

"Greta and I will work it out," said Tyler. Greta was in Girl Scouts, and Tyler was good at woodwork.

Greta beamed. "You guys just relax," she said. "And we'll take care of it."

24

DON'T THINK IT'S *NATURAL*," SAID HENRY.

"You're just nervous," said Nicola. "It's perfectly safe."

She and the rest of the Space Brigade were sitting together on the raft that Tyler and Greta had constructed. It was made of varying lengths of branch and tied together firmly with vine. Although it was a bit rough-looking, it did the job perfectly and was bobbing around merrily on the river. Nicola thought Tyler and Greta had done an amazing job (and judging by the pride on both their faces, so did they). The only problem was that Henry was refusing to climb aboard.

"I expect your roft will sink the moment I get on," he said. "I know I appear skinny but I have very heavy bones!"

"It's a raft, not a roft, and it won't sink," said Greta unsympathetically. "Just hurry up and get on!"

But Henry seemed frozen on the spot, just like Nicola had been before she went scuba diving.

He needed a reason to move.

Nicola said loudly to Katie, "Look at the way the moonlight creates a pathway over there! Wouldn't that make a lovely painting!"

Out of the corner of her eye, Nicola saw Henry craning his head to see the moonlit pathway.

Katie caught on right away. "Oh, yes, and the contrast between the grainy texture of the raft against the water is so . . . um, *visually interesting.*"

Henry didn't hesitate. He waded purposefully through the water toward the raft. "I must see that contrast!"

"On you hop, then." Sean dragged him up onto the raft.

"Oh, yes, I see what you mean." Henry lay down on his stomach to examine the water against the wood. "That is lovely! If I only had my sketch—oh my, we appear to be moving!"

The Space Brigade had all picked up the makeshift oars they had created out of tree branches and were paddling furiously.

The raft sped off bumpily down the river. It rocked around a lot, and Nicola noticed water was seeping through the gaps in between the branches, but apart from that it was quite stable.

"Well done, you two," she said to Tyler and Greta.

"Thank you," said Tyler.

"Yes, well, that's why I think everyone should be a Girl or Boy Scout," said Greta. "It should be a *requirement* of Space

Brigade membership. It teaches you so many useful skills."

"Goodness! We're moving so quickly! The shore is just *whipping* by! I've never experienced a sensation like it!" Henry Sweet sat up in the middle of the raft with an enchanted expression on his face like a toddler on a merry-go-round. "We'll reach Griddlemill in no time! We're moving—and yet my legs are still!"

"Can I ask you a question, Henry?" said Tyler.

"Certainly!" said Henry agreeably.

"Has your planet invented the wheel?"

Henry frowned. "The wheel? Wheels?"

Tyler struggled to explain what he meant. "It's like a circular, ah, disc—and it spins on an axis. It's sort of the basis of all transport."

"That sounds like a very interesting object," said Henry, obviously trying to be polite.

"You really need to invent the wheel," said Tyler. "It would change everything."

"Yes, well, we'll certainly look into it," said Henry vaguely. "Oh, my goodness, we must be going by the Village of Song already! Listen! They sing throughout the night and sleep through the day."

They listened, and an angelic sound filled the night air. It sounded like a young boy's voice holding one high, sweet note. It was so unbelievably pure it gave Nicola goosebumps. Then other voices joined in, their voices harmonizing to create a rainbow of sound.

Katie dropped her oar on the raft. Tears rolled down her face.

"I must go there," she said. "I have to go there!"

She dived off the side of the raft and began to swim toward the shore.

"Katie!" shrieked Nicola. "What are you *doing*?"

"Ah, well, if she appreciates music, that's the last you'll see of her," said Henry. "Music appreciators find it impossible to leave the Village of Song. Your friend will grow old there."

Without a word, Sean and Shimlara dropped their oars and dived into the river to bring her back.

"Leave me alone!" cried Katie, when she saw them coming after her. "I must get to that music!"

"Stuff her ears with leaves!" called out Henry, as the sound of singing grew even louder. "It's the only way!"

Shimlara scooped up some leaves floating by, grabbed Katie, and pushed them into her ears.

"No, no! I must hear it! Let me hear it!"

"I'm sorry! I'm sorry!" Shimlara was almost crying, as Katie fought against her like a drowning person.

"It's for your own good," said Sean, grabbing Katie in the lifesaving hold.

He and Shimlara dragged Katie back onto the raft.

"Paddle!" ordered Nicola, when everyone was back on board. She wanted to get away from the singing. The more she heard, the more she began to think it would be an excellent idea to jump in and swim to the Village of Song herself. She and Katie could go together and spend the rest of their lives doing nothing but listening to the blissful sound of—*No! Stop thinking like that! You would never see your family again!*

Water flew as everyone paddled like crazy. The raft flew around a bend in the river. The sound of singing grew fainter and finally vanished altogether.

Katie sat up and pulled the leaves from her ears.

"I'm sorry," she said sheepishly. "I don't know what came over me."

"I'm sorry for being so rough with you," said Shimlara.

"Oh, no, *I'm* sorry for putting you in such a difficult situation," said Katie.

"And *I'm* sorry I have to listen to you girls go on and on about how sorry you are," said Sean.

"Are there any more villages like that coming up?" Nicola asked Henry.

"No," said Henry. "The river will make its way through the Sublime Mountains and then we'll be in Griddlemill."

They spent the next few hours quietly paddling their

way down the river, their arms beginning to ache from the effort.

"How are you going to rescue the Gorgioskios from the prison camp?" asked Henry at one point.

"We don't know," admitted Nicola. "We'll work something out once we see what we're up against."

Henry nodded. He was lying on his back close to the edge of the raft and letting one hand trail through the water. It didn't seem to have occurred to him to offer to help out with the paddling.

"How are you going to win the war against Volcomania?" Sean asked Henry.

Henry blinked. "Well, I expect we're going to lose. I don't really see there's much point in even trying. Those Volcomanians are really a rather *rough* sort of people."

"That's not the right attitude," said Sean. "Are you a man or a mouse?"

"I believe I'm a man," said Henry confusedly. "What's a mouse?"

But there was no time for Sean to explain because the river had suddenly changed its nature, like a quiet person losing their temper. It was no longer meandering peacefully through the mountains. It was a raging torrent of white water.

"Why didn't you warn us, Henry?" cried Nicola over

the roar of the water, as her oar was snatched from her grasp and the raft was flung around like a flimsy piece of driftwood.

"About what?" called back Henry.

"About *this*!"

"I always wanted to go white-water rafting!" shouted Sean joyously, as if he were on a roller-coaster ride.

"Well, I didn't!" yelled back Nicola.

The raft flew into the air and crashed down again, only just missing being smashed to smithereens against the side of a boulder.

Bumpity-bumpity-BUMP!

Bumpity-bumpity-BUMP!

Nicola felt as though she were being tossed around like a carrot in a stir-fry.

"Forget paddling!" yelled Tyler. *"Just hold on!"*

25

**ILENCE. STILLNESS. THE SCENT OF ROSES.**

Nicola tentatively opened her eyes. Had they really survived that? Her memories of the last ten minutes of her life seemed to be broken into tiny pieces, like jagged fragments of glass.

She could remember:

Clinging to the side of the raft as it flew high in the air.

The feel of cold water closing over her head as her side of the raft tipped under.

Gasping for air as it righted itself.

The sound of Sean hollering "WOO-HOO" as if he were actually having a good time.

And then suddenly it was all over. The roaring sound stopped. The raft became wonderfully still.

Nicola sat up. The rest of the Space Brigade and Henry were all lying flat on their backs on the raft. Everyone was drenched through. The mountains were behind them and the river had widened. It was now flat and tranquil. The raft was barely moving. Above them, the sky was becoming lighter and the stars were fading.

"Dawn," said Henry Sweet, sitting up. "My favorite

time of the day." He looked at Nicola. "Have you ever seen a Whimsian dawn?"

Nicola shook her head.

"You're about to see something you'll never forget." Nicola could see the curve of Whimsy's giant sun glimmering on the horizon. The light began to change. Everything was bathed in a fine gold mist, as if someone was sprinkling the planet with gold dust. Streaks of peach, cherry, and mango slowly appeared across the sky, as if that same person was now lazily trying out paint colors on a canvas. As the sun rose higher, the colors deepened and became more beautiful, like an orchestra reaching its crescendo.

By the time the sun was hovering over the horizon like a burning coin, Whimsy's birds were singing and the Space Brigade were all sitting up, lifting their faces to the soft, warm rays.

Henry raised his eyebrows at Nicola.

"Incredible," she agreed.

"My life's goal is to paint a Whimsy dawn," he said. "I've tried it a hundred times but I never quite capture its essence. One day I will."

"Unless Volcomania wins the war," said Nicola.

"What do you mean?" said Henry. "I'll still paint! Painting is my life! I would never stop. I paint every day of my life."

"Yes, but if Volcomania wins the war, everyone will be put in artistic factories. You'll have to paint what they tell you to paint. You'll be on a schedule."

"A *schedule*? Me? I couldn't paint to a schedule!"

"You might have to," said Nicola. She didn't mean to be cruel. She just wanted Henry to understand what this war could mean to his planet.

"That's why you have to fight," said Sean.

"That's why you have to *defend* yourselves," said Nicola.

Henry stared at them. His mouth opened as if he were going to say something but no sound came out.

"Is this Griddlemill?" interrupted Shimlara. "I can smell the roses."

Henry cleared his throat and looked around. He pointed at the shore, where dozens of rosebushes were growing. "That's Griddlemill there. There's a beautiful picnic spot through—oh. Oh dear." He dropped his hand.

"What is it?" said Nicola.

She looked where he'd been pointing and saw an ugly tangle of vicious-looking barbed wire rising high in the air above the roses.

"They've built a prison camp over our picnic area," said Henry. "That's where I proposed to my wife!" He leaped to his feet, causing the raft to rock alarmingly. "These people are barbarians! They must be stopped!"

"Now you're talking," said Sean.

Henry took off his beret and crushed it between his hands. "I will defeat them single-handedly!"

"See now, that's just silly," said Greta.

"But I have *right* on my side!" cried Henry. He punched both fists over his head and then lost his balance completely and fell straight back into the river.

He came up spluttering water and clambered back on the raft. He wiped his face with his beret and looked sheepish.

"I'm just not sure where to start," he admitted. "Where do you think I should start? Could you help? Have any of you ever won a war before?"

The Space Brigade all shook their heads and Henry looked dejected.

"You've got to play to their weaknesses, while using your strengths," said Nicola, remembering something her dad had said while watching a football game on television.

Henry brightened.

"Right! Yes, of course! So our strengths are music, art, literature, and theater. Their strengths are that they're organized and methodical and quite violent, with lots of weapons and bombs, and their weaknesses are—their weaknesses are—mmmmm. They don't seem to have any weaknesses."

BRIIIIIIIIIIIIIIIIIIIIIIIIIIIIIIIIIIIIIIIIIIIIIIIIIIIIIIIIIIIIIING!

A sound like a tremendously loud alarm clock shattered the peaceful morning.

Henry clapped his hands over his ears. "What is that awful sound?"

"It's coming from the prison camp," said Shimlara.

There was a hollow sound like someone lifting up a megaphone and a harsh, authoritarian voice rang out.

"Wake up, prisoners! All prisoners are ordered to report for work duty. There will be no breakfast this morning due to the bad conduct of Prisoner Georgio Gorgioskio!"

"Oh no," said Shimlara. "Typical! Dad is in trouble! Come on! We've got to get them out of there."

26

**ICOLA'S HEART THUMPED AS THEY PULLED THE**
raft up onto the riverbank about a half a mile
away from the prison camp. They had agreed
that if they were approached by anyone they
would stick with their story of being Earthling journalists reporting on the war. However, first they
wanted to do a thorough inspection of the camp.

They hid their raft under a pile of rose petals. The air
was thick with the sweet smell of roses, but there were
other, less fragrant scents as well.

"I think it's boiled potatoes," said Sean, sniffing the air.
"And gunpowder. Maybe sweaty socks?"

"How dare they ruin the famous scent of Griddlemill!"
said Henry. "Quick! Let us hurry!"

Henry seemed to be changing. His eyes were more
focused and less dreamy, his manner more decisive. Nicola
thought perhaps he was acting more like a president, until
he suddenly pounced on a perfectly ordinary rose petal
lying on the ground.

"Why, just look at the enchanting shape of this petal!"
he cried.

"Enchanting," agreed Sean, pulling on his sleeve. "But we've sort of got things to do."

"Oh, yes, yes, of course." Henry carefully put the petal in his pocket.

The rose bushes provided the perfect cover as they carefully made their way back along the river shore as close as they dared to the prison camp. Two Volcomanian soldiers were guarding the gates to the camp, standing very still and straight, like the guards at Buckingham Palace.

Nicola silently pointed away from the river toward the back of the camp. The rest of the Space Brigade nodded in agreement.

They crept around the barbed wire fence, trying not to make a sound. It was difficult, because they had to weave their way through overgrown rose bushes. The fragrance was beautiful, but the thorns were sharp against their skin.

Once they were far enough away from the guards, Nicola stopped and everyone tried to see through the fence without cutting themselves on the barbed wire.

Nicola could see the prisoners lining up in rows. Their hair was unwashed, their clothes filthy, and they all looked miserable, tired, and hungry. Nicola searched the faces for Shimlara's family.

"Prisoners!" boomed a fat Volcomanian guard. He was

standing in front of the prisoners, with his legs spread and his stomach pushed out. He reminded Nicola of Jeffrey Snog, the bully back at their school on Earth.

Sean was obviously thinking the same thing. "He could be related to Jeffrey Snog," he whispered in Nicola's ear.

"I'm sure you're all anxious to know how you'll be spending your day!" shouted the guard. "Wonderful news! You have an interesting day ahead of you! I know how you enjoyed polishing our boots yesterday. Guess what? Today you will be polishing the barbed wire fence! Of course, you may suffer a few nasty cuts but I'm sure you'll take pride in the appearance of your camp!"

"Excuse me!" said one of the prisoners.

Nicola heard a quick intake of breath from Shimlara. The prisoner stepped forward and Nicola saw that it was Shimlara's dad, Georgio. He looked thin and exhausted, and his famous bristly mustache was drooping, but he still held his head high.

"What is it *this* time, Gorgioskio?" sighed the fat guard.

"Good morning! Isn't it a lovely day! And may I say you're looking very well this morning, sir! Have you lost weight?"

The guard frowned and looked at his huge belly with uncertainty.

"Perhaps a little."

"I thought so!" said Georgio. "Now, although I'd *love* nothing more than to cut my hands to shreds polishing the barbed wire fence today, the thing is, the Interplanetary Guidelines for Prisoners of War expressly forbids it. According to Clause Twenty-Five B, prisoners shall not be required to clean their own prison camp. I don't think Mrs. Mania would be happy if she heard you were going against the Interplanetary Convention."

The fat guard looked uncertain. "I don't know about that."

"I suggest you give us all a nice rest day," said Georgio. "Or better still, why not let us all go free? And while you're at it, why not forget this silly war altogether?"

Suddenly the fat guard was furious, as if he'd been tricked.

"Gorgioskio! Solitary confinement for you!"

Georgio groaned. "The thing is I find solitary confinement so horribly solitary! Do you think you could join me there and we could play a nice game of cards? I'd let you win!"

The guard looked tempted by the offer. Then his face changed. "Stop trying to confuse me! You're going to solitary confinement!"

Suddenly Mully appeared by her husband's side.

"Mom," said Shimlara under her breath.

"Do you think you could send me to solitary confinement in my husband's place?" she asked politely. "I'm afraid he'll lose his mind if you send him there again. He can't stand being alone."

"This is a prison camp, not a day spa!" The guard stamped his foot. "You're not meant to be enjoying yourselves!" He gestured at a group of Volcomanian guards standing to attention next to him. "Take him to solitary confinement! And do *not* under any circumstances play cards with him!"

As he was from the planet of Globagaskar, Georgio was about double the height of the Volcomanians. It took six burly guards to carry him off and Georgio didn't make it easy for them.

There was a sudden commotion as Shimlara's little brother ran out from the prisoners. "Don't you touch my daddy!" he cried, swatting at the guards with his hands.

Nicola held her breath.

"Oh, Squid, honey, don't," said Shimlara softly. Nicola turned her head and saw that there were tears running down her friend's face.

For the first time Georgio looked frightened. "Go back to your mom, Squid," he said. "Daddy is fine."

Mully ran out and scooped Squid up in her arms.

"I've had it up to *here* with you lot!" yelled the fat guard.

He indicated the middle of his forehead with a chubby hand. "I'm going to have a nap! By the time I wake up, I want to see that barbed wire fence *gleaming*!"

He stomped off. Meanwhile the remaining guards handed out buckets and rags, and the prisoners slowly shuffled off with slumped shoulders to begin cleaning the fence.

The Space Brigade turned to look at one another.

Nicola put a finger over her lips and they crept away from the camp.

"I have never seen such *evil*!" said Henry Sweet.

"We've got to rescue *all* those poor prisoners!" said Katie. "Not just the Gorgioskios!"

"That's what Dad says, too," said Shimlara.

"What do you mean?" said Nicola with surprise.

"I spoke to him telepathically," said Shimlara.

"Ah," said Nicola. She'd quite forgotten that Shimlara would be able to read her father's mind once he was in her sight.

"He was pretty happy to hear we're here," said Shimlara. "He was thinking so fast, I could barely understand him! He purposely got himself put in solitary confinement so that we could all talk to him. He said to go around to the back right-hand corner of the camp."

"What else did he say?" asked Nicola.

Shimlara looked at Henry.

"He said the only way to ensure we didn't end up captured, too, was to help Henry Sweet and his people win the war against Volcomania."

Henry paled. "Goodness me."

27

PSSST! DAD? ARE YOU THERE?"

Shimlara stood with her hands on her hips at the far corner of the prison camp fence.

"He said the solitary confinement cell was underground. It's built into a wall of rock just outside the perimeter of the camp," she said to the others. "I'm just not sure where—what's that?"

They all stopped to listen. A tiny, faraway voice seemed to be coming from beneath their feet.

"Under here!"

Tyler fell to his knees near the barbed-wire fence. He cleared away some dirt with the palm of his hand to reveal a small iron grille in the ground. Georgio was peering up at them, his dark eyes flashing with excitement. He was sitting with his knees squashed close to his chest in a small, dark underground cell.

"Look at all your lovely, dear faces! Nicola! Sean! Tyler! Katie! Greta! I've never been so happy to see you all!" he cried. "When I heard Shimlara's voice in my head, I nearly jumped out of my skin. Oh, and you've got Henry Sweet with you! Hello, Mr. Sweet! It's a pleasure to see you again.

How is the war progressing? We don't get to hear much here, obviously. I'm sorry, I'm talking so much, but solitary confinement does seem to mess with my mind, and I've only been here five minutes. Last time they put me in here for a day! When I came out I spoke for two hours straight without taking a breath! Drove your mother crazy! I never realized how important human interaction was to me!"

"Dad," said Shimlara.

"And of course, I get so *bored*, and you know how I can't stand to be bored! I try to set myself little mental challenges, but to be honest—"

"Dad!" said Shimlara.

"Sorry," said Georgio humbly. "How are you, honey?"

"I'm fine," said Shimlara. "Are you all right? Are Mom and Squid okay?"

Her voice cracked. She was obviously trying not to cry. Nicola tried to imagine how she would feel seeing her dad locked away in a tiny prison cell.

"Oh, yes, yes, we're all fine. It's not exactly a dream vacation but . . ." His words drifted away.

"Shhh. Someone is coming," he whispered.

The Space Brigade stepped away from the grille and fell silent.

They heard the sound of bars being rattled.

"Feeling hungry, are you, Gorgioskio?" said a rough voice.

"Well, yes, I am quite peckish," answered Georgio amiably.

"That's good, because I've got some nice crispy bacon, sizzling sausages, and fried eggs for your breakfast!"

"Sounds delicious!" said Georgio.

"*Ha ha ha!* That's what *I'm* having for breakfast. You know what you're having! *Air!* That should fill you up, eh? See ya, Gorgioskio!"

The voice trailed off. Georgio looked back up at them. "They've got quite a sense of humor, these Volcomanians," he said dryly.

"They're horrible!" said Shimlara. "We're going to get you and Mom and Squid out of there today!"

"That's very nice of you all, but as I said, we really need you to rescue *all* the prisoners," said Georgio. "We couldn't leave anyone behind! Do you know they've got the *United Aunts* in here? We're sharing a cell with them! When the intergalactic community hears about this, Volcomania is going to be the most unpopular planet in the galaxy."

"I don't care about the other prisoners!" Shimlara stamped her foot in frustration. "I only care about rescuing you!"

"And how were you planning to do that?" said Georgio.

"We're pretending to be journalists from Earth," said

Nicola. "We thought we'd act like we're doing a story on the prison camp and—what's that?"

Georgio was pushing a rolled-up piece of paper up through the bars of the grille. "You might want to look at this," he said.

Nicola took the piece of paper and unrolled it. It seemed to be some sort of notice or flyer. The others gathered around her to read it.

It said:

WANTED! DEAD OR ALIVE!
TWO MILLION GOLD BAR REWARD FOR CAPTURE!

A group of Earthlings, accompanied by one Globagaskarian, are pretending to be journalists for the purposes of undermining Volcomania's sensible, necessary war on the hopeless planet of Whimsy. **THEY ARE NOT JOURNALISTS**. They are, in fact, the infamous Space Brigade. The Space Brigade is responsible for **MANY CRIMES**, including:

★ The kidnapping of Globagaskar's dear little Princess Petronella.

★ Inciting a rebellion on the planet of Shobble leading to the downfall of the kind, gentle commander in chief, Enrico Aloisio.

Since arriving on Volcomania, these hardened criminals have already been responsible for duping police and allowing evil war protesters to escape. It is believed they have traveled to the planet of Whimsy to cause further trouble. If seen, they should be approached with caution and large weapons. Use any force necessary to contain them.

—— **BY PERSONAL ORDER OF MRS. MANIA** ——

There was a grainy, black-and-white photo on the flyer. Someone in the Secret Service must have taken it when they were getting on the bus after Mrs. Mania had turned up.

It was an extremely unflattering photo. They all seemed to have shifty, criminal expressions on their faces. Even Katie, who was the nicest person Nicola knew, had her mouth pulled down in a sour snarl.

"This makes us seem *horrible*," cried Nicola. "If I read it, I would think we were seriously bad."

"Yeah, we really look like 'hardened criminals,'" said Sean happily, as if it were a great thing.

"Did you really do all that stuff?" asked Henry Sweet nervously.

"Yes," admitted Nicola.

Henry took a few steps back.

"But you see, we *needed* to kidnap Princess Petronella," said Nicola. "Because she was going to destroy Earth."

"Oh, and just for your interest, she's not exactly a 'dear little' princess," commented Sean.

"And the commander in chief of Shobble was *not* kind or gentle," said Katie.

"Yes, but—"

"No need to worry, Henry," said Georgio. "They're good kids."

"So we can't pretend to be a news crew anymore," said Nicola. She was disappointed. She had been looking forward to doing some more interviewing.

"Your only option is to help the Whimsians win the war against Volcomania," said Georgio. "Otherwise someone will capture you for the reward."

"We're not *soldiers*, Dad," said Shimlara. "We don't know how to win a war!"

"The Space Brigade had no experience at all before the last two missions and look at what you've achieved," said Georgio. "I have every confidence in you!"

"Dad, this isn't Saturday morning sports," said Shimlara. "You can't just give one of your little pep talks like you do before a space-ball game."

"It's *just* like Saturday morning sports! Your competitors are the Volcomanians. How are you going to beat them? You need strategies! A plan! Oh, and a little trickery is perfectly acceptable. You're creative people! The Whimsians are creative people! Aren't you, Henry?"

"Yes, we are!" cried Henry. His face was flushed with hope. "We can do it!" He seemed to be the only one who was feeling inspired by Georgio.

"Oh, and one other thing. We've heard that Mrs. Mania is planning to visit Whimsy and inspect the camp," said Georgio. "That's why they're getting the prisoners to clean the barbed wire fence. So that's the perfect time for you to launch your attack."

"Launch our attack?" said Nicola faintly.

"Yes! I think you should capture Mrs. Mania! In all the war histories I've read, capturing your opponent's leader works out beautifully. You could *lure* her into your clutches with, umm, I don't know—some sort of nice food?"

"She's not a puppy dog!" Shimlara rolled her eyes. "We really need to get some advice from Mom about this. She's the one with the war experience."

Georgio looked hurt. "I know I haven't fought in a war, but I have read numerous books and seen a lot—"

"When is Mrs. Mania coming to inspect the camp?" interrupted Nicola.

Before Georgio got to answer, there was the sound of heavy footsteps. The Space Brigade hastily stepped back.

"Gorgioskio!" called out the same nasty voice as before. "Got a treat for you! We're having a cleanup. You're the only one tall enough to dust the top shelves!"

"Ah, glad to be of help!" Georgio answered. "Cleaning up for Mrs. Mania's visit, are you? *Her visit tomorrow morning at eight a.m.?!*"

"That's none of your business," said the rough voice. There was a scraping sound of keys in a lock. "Come on, out you come!" Their voices vanished.

The Space Brigade and Henry Sweet were all looking at their watches. They had less than twenty-four hours to work out how to win a war and capture a president.

28

THIS IS WHERE I KISSED MY WIFE FOR THE FIRST time," said Henry Sweet, dreamily. "Her lips tasted like strawberries. They were as soft as—"

"Too much information!" Sean clapped his hands over his ears.

Henry had led them to a giant tree a short walk away from the prison camp. The tree was beautiful, with low branches laden with strange flowers that smelled like honey. Its trunk's circumference was the size of a swimming pool. Henry had walked over to the trunk and found his initials and those of his wife carved deep into the bark. He had slid his hand straight down from the carving and suddenly the bark had given way to reveal a small opening, just large enough for them all to crawl through.

Nicola gasped with surprise when she saw the inside of the trunk. It was like being inside a secret cave. The light was dim and green. The ground was soft and springy. Tiny butterflies fluttered above their heads like falling blossoms.

"What a romantic place for your first kiss," sighed Katie.

"Is anyone else *really* hungry?" said Sean loudly.

Everyone sighed. They hadn't eaten anything since the sugary desserts the night before.

"I liked the sound of that breakfast the horrible Volcomanian guard was describing," said Tyler. "Bacon, eggs, sausages!"

Nicola's mouth watered.

"We don't have time to think about food," she said briskly. "We've got to work out a plan."

"I don't think I can concentrate without breakfast," said Sean.

"You're going to have to!" Nicola was feeling extremely irritable.

"I wonder if the Griddlemill Café still delivers," said Henry. "They used to do a lovely hot breakfast. My wife had a fondness for their buttermilk pancakes with maple syrup. You just whistle three times like a Melody Bird and they send a waitress to take your order."

"Why didn't you mention this earlier!" said Sean. "Start whistling!"

Henry went to the entrance of the tree, pushed aside the bark, pursed his lips, and whistled a melodious tune.

He came back inside the tree and sat down. "Of course, they might have closed down due to the war," he said.

Nicola quietly crossed her fingers. She saw Sean bite his lip and Katie close her eyes.

A minute passed. Nobody said a word.

"Looks like they might have closed down," said Henry regretfully.

Another minute passed.

"Okay, well, let's get to work," said Nicola, faint with disappointment and hunger. "So, we need—"

The bark twitched and a young girl with long chestnut braids and liquid brown eyes walked into their hideaway. She spoke in a fast, bored monotone. "Hi-my-name-is-Poppy. I'll-be-your-waitress-today-may-I-take-your-order?" She pulled a pencil out from behind her ear and a notepad from the pocket of her white apron and looked up at them expectantly.

"Are we pleased to see *you*!" said Sean.

"Sorry I took a while," said Poppy. "I was working on a new monologue."

"Monologue? Are you an actress?" asked Katie.

"Acting is my life, my passion, my destiny!" said Poppy dramatically. "I can do *any* voice with perfect pitch. Do you want me to show you?"

"Sure."

"Are we pleased to see *you*!" said Poppy in an absolutely perfect imitation of Sean.

Everyone laughed and applauded except for Sean, who said sourly, "Great. Well done. So, I'm thinking crispy sausages."

"All we've got is the Breakfast Special—bacon, eggs, sausages, toast, and waffles—sound okay? I'm only meant to serve it to Volcomanians but I'll make an exception. You all look so hungry."

They ordered seven breakfast specials.

"How much?" asked Nicola, hoping they had enough Whimsian currency.

"It's free." Poppy waved away their money.

She looked them up and down. "You're Earthlings, aren't you?"

"We're a news crew—" began Nicola uncertainly, wondering if their cover was now totally blown.

"*Sure* you are." Poppy grinned broadly and winked. She had obviously read the "Wanted" notice that Georgio had shown them. "And I'm the president of Whimsy."

"Actually, *I'm* the president of Whimsy," said Henry.

"Oh, are you?" said Poppy. "I didn't even know we had one."

A short time later she was back carrying a tray piled high with wonderful-smelling food.

"Do you deliver meals to the Volcomanian soldiers in the prison camp?" asked Nicola.

"Yes," said Poppy. "Why?"

"You might be able to help us," said Nicola, although she wasn't sure how.

"Just let me know what I can do," said Poppy.

She left, and they all settled down to enjoy crispy bacon, succulent sausages, fluffy eggs, and featherlight waffles.

Thank goodness for food, thought Nicola. Then she remembered all those prisoners cleaning the barbed wire fence without breakfast and felt guilty. As soon as they were all released she would make sure to arrange all the food they could eat.

They all sat in deep silence for a while, either looking at their empty plates or watching the movement of the butterflies fluttering around them.

Sean stretched his arms above his head. "All that food has made me sleepy."

Sleepy. Somebody had been talking about something that caused sleepiness just recently. Who was it?

"Aha!" Nicola jerked up her head and pointed at Sean.

"What?" Sean looked over his shoulders with alarm. "Spider? Snake?"

"I've got an idea."

"So do I!" said Katie. "It has to do with that waitress."

"And me too!" said Tyler. "It's about using Whimsy's strengths."

"Actually I think I've got an idea to do with that, too!" cried Sean.

The food had done the trick. Now that they all had full stomachs, their minds were sharp again. Suddenly everyone was on their feet, talking at the same time, ideas sparking off other ideas, and even the butterflies seemed energized by the electric new atmosphere.

29

T WAS EIGHT A.M. THE NEXT MORNING. AND THE
Space Brigade and Henry Sweet were hiding behind
a rosebush outside the prison gates.

They were all tired and a bit snappy. They hadn't
slept at all the night before. Instead, they had spent
the whole night in the tree trunk working out a plan to win
the war against Volcomania.

If it worked, Volcomania would be defeated by nightfall.

If it failed, the Space Brigade would be in chains by
nightfall.

Their plan was audacious, complicated, and possibly
ridiculous. Nicola really had no idea if it was going to be a
spectacular success or a spectacular failure.

"Here they come!" said Greta. "Right on time."

Nicola looked up just as Mrs. Mania's limousine was
driving through the gates of the prison camp. It was the
same one they'd seen on Volcomania.

"Didn't they have to scuba dive? How do they get that
car through the Underground Sea?" she asked.

"It converts to a submarine," answered Tyler.

"How do you know that?" asked Nicola.

"It was obvious," said Tyler. "The tires were wet, the windows were all foggy, and they left the periscope up on the roof."

"Right," said Nicola, who hadn't noticed any of that.

A few minutes later they saw Poppy, their waitress from the day before, walk into the camp pushing an enormous trolley piled high with covered plates of food. She was biting her lip and her eyes were darting all over the place.

"She looks nervous," said Shimlara. "So much for being a great actress!"

"They won't even notice; they'll be too busy looking at the food," Sean reassured her.

Poppy disappeared into the camp. Ten nail-biting minutes passed and suddenly she came running back out. Nicola's heart sank when she saw the terrified expression on her face. Something must have gone wrong.

"What is it?" asked Nicola fearfully. "What happened? Didn't it work?"

"It was all going beautifully," said Poppy. "They all got into the food right away and within a few minutes they were falling sound asleep!"

It had been Nicola's idea to grind rose petals into the food Poppy took into the camp. She had remembered how Henry Sweet's wife had said the rose petals were a cure for insomnia. Once the guards and Mrs. Mania were fast asleep, they would go into the camp and restrain them.

"So what's the problem?" asked Sean. "That's what we wanted!"

"Yes, but one person hasn't eaten anything at all. She's wide awake!"

Disaster. "It's not Mrs. Mania, is it?" asked Katie.

"No, she's sound asleep! It's worse! It's that really tall princess with the—" She stopped. "Why are you all laughing? I'm telling you, this girl looks scary!"

"That's our friend, Princess Petronella," explained Nicola. "And she's not as scary as she looks. Don't worry— we'll take it from here. Thanks for all your help. Don't forget, we'll need you later!"

Poppy had two important roles to play in the execution of their plan.

"No problem," said Poppy with a smile, and ran off.

"Let's get in there fast before they wake up," said Nicola to the others.

"This is so thrilling!" cried Henry Sweet as they ran in the prison gates. "The ups! The downs! The terror! The joy!" He tripped and nearly stumbled.

"Just concentrate on what you're *doing*, Henry," said Greta. "Instead of constantly thinking about how you're *feeling*."

For once, Nicola was in complete agreement with Greta.

It was strange entering *into* a prison camp, when Nicola's every instinct told her to run in the other direction. At first, the place seemed silent and deserted. There were no guards or prisoners in sight.

Then Nicola heard a familiar voice.

"I *knew* it! I must be the smartest person in the galaxy!"

It was Princess Petronella, standing at the doorway of a building beneath a sign saying FOOD HALL.

"Hi! How are you?" called out Nicola, filled with sudden affection for the princess. There was something comforting about seeing her familiar, self-absorbed face in these frightening surroundings.

"I'm a genius," answered the princess seriously. "I have amazing powers of observation! I noticed that the girl delivering the food looked nervous and I said to myself, *I bet that food is poisoned.* Then I thought, *I bet the Space Brigade is behind it*! So I didn't touch a crumb, even though I'm famished! Just when I think I couldn't be any smarter, I outdo myself!"

"You're so modest, too," said Sean.

"It's nice to see you again, Princess Petronella," said Katie.

"Yes, I imagine it would be very nice for you," said the

princess. "Tell me, what poison have you used? Are they all about to die painful deaths?"

Nicola and the others walked into the dining hall and looked around curiously. A number of tables had been set up for breakfast. There was a big sign at one end saying,

THE VOLCOMANIAN PRISON CAMP WELCOMES
OUR FINE AND CLEVER PRESIDENT, MRS. MANIA!

The room was perfectly silent, except for the low rumbling sound of people snoring.

Everywhere Nicola looked she could see sleeping guards. Some of them had fallen asleep on their breakfast plates, cheeks comfortably cushioned on sausages. Others were sitting upright in their chairs, heads tipped back, mouths wide open, and forks still gripped in their hands. The horrible guard who had reminded Sean and Nicola of the school bully had landed face-first in his scrambled eggs, where he was snoring like a snuffly pig.

At the end of the hall was a raised platform with a long table that had obviously been set up for the guests of honor. Mrs. Mania was sleeping peacefully with her head cradled in her arms. She didn't look at all forbidding when she was asleep—in fact, she looked quite nice. On her left was her son, who was sleeping with his chin on his chest, his hands still clutching his knife and fork. On Mrs. Mania's right was an empty chair with an untouched plate of food that was obviously Princess Petronella's.

"They're just sleeping," Nicola explained to Princess Petronella. "They're not going to die violent deaths."

"Oh good," said Princess Petronella. "I would have been quite disappointed to see Marty Mania die." She pointed at Mrs. Mania's sleeping son. "He might look like a toad, but I've become quite fond of him. I've decided to add him to my collection of 'friends.' I've got so many now! I might actually need to cut back."

She narrowed her eyes at the Space Brigade as if trying to decide which of her friends she didn't need.

"Oh, by the way, this is the president of Whimsy!" Nicola awkwardly gestured at Henry Sweet. She was always forgetting the right way to introduce people. "Ah, Henry Sweet, this is Princess Petronella. Princess Petronella, Henry Sweet."

"I am honored to meet you," said Henry with a sweeping bow.

"You certainly are," agreed Princess Petronella with a sniff.

"Ah, Nicola, we'd better not chat for too long," Sean reminded her. "We haven't got long before they start waking up."

"Yes, you're right," said Nicola. "Let's go, everybody!" Everyone pulled out coils of rope from their bags. (They had gotten the rope from Poppy the waitress's mother. She had been a tightrope artist before her arthritis started acting up.)

The night before, Greta had trained them all on various knots she had learned at Girl Scouts, such as the Double Fisherman's Knot. Today they were using the skills to tie each guard securely to a chair.

It was hard work. The guards were big people and they were sleeping so deeply their arms and legs were floppy and heavy.

Nicola's fingers ached and beads of sweat formed on her forehead. Henry had estimated that it would take about an hour before the effects of the rose petals wore off and people started to wake up. They had thought that would be plenty of time.

"We're never going to finish before they wake up," said Shimlara desperately from the front of the room, where she was tying up the sleeping Mrs. Mania.

"If only we had more people to help," agreed Greta.

"You've got plenty of people who would be more than happy to help," commented Princess Petronella, who wasn't being much help herself, relaxing in a chair with her feet up on one of the tables.

"What do you mean?" said Nicola, and then she slapped herself lightly on the forehead.

She went through the pocket of the sleeping guard she was tying up and found a heavy set of keys.

"We need to release the prisoners!"

30

RELEASING THE PRISONERS WAS A WONDERFUL experience.

They were being held in a narrow concrete building. Each tiny, dark, damp cell held so many prisoners, they had to sit in rows with their knees held tightly to their chests. Some of them were scaly-skinned Volcomanians who must have been protesting against the war. Others were beautiful Whimsians, who must have done something to annoy the invading army.

When Nicola unlocked each gate, the prisoners stared up at her without saying a word, their eyes dull and dirty, their thin faces full of sad resignation, assuming she was just another guard. When she said, "You're free!" they were transformed. First there was shock and disbelief, followed by relief and delight. Some of them whooped with joy. Others cried with happiness and wanted to hug Nicola.

"Hurry! Hurry!" she told them. "We need your help!" As Nicola unlocked each cell, the rest of the Space Brigade led the prisoners away to help with tying up the guards.

Shimlara had been craning over Nicola's shoulder,

looking for her family. Finally she found them in the very last cell. With their long Globagaskarian legs, they looked especially uncomfortable in the cramped conditions. Squid had his thumb in his mouth and his head resting against his mother's shoulder. Mully had her eyes closed as she leaned against the back wall of the cell. Georgio, who had obviously been released from solitary confinement, was sitting next to his wife and son with his forehead resting on his kneecaps.

It was Squid who caught sight of Shimlara first. He took his thumb out of his mouth and grinned widely at his big sister.

"Shimlara," he said clearly.

"Yes, darling," said Mully tiredly, without opening her eyes. "We'll see Shimlara soon, I promise."

"You can see me right now," said Shimlara.

Mully's eyes flew open. Georgio's head jerked up like a jack-in-the-box.

"Shimlara!" cried Mully.

Nicola unlocked the gate and the prisoners all got to their feet with difficulty and walked out into the corridor.

"I told you we'd be out of here soon!" said Georgio triumphantly. He clapped one of the other prisoners who had been sharing their cell on the shoulder. "That's my daughter I was telling you about!"

"I must admit I was rather beginning to think she was a figment of your imagination," smiled the prisoner, a short, fuzzy-haired lady with pink apple cheeks. She didn't look like she was from Volcomania or the planet of Whimsy. She wasn't an Earthling, but for some reason she seemed slightly familiar to Nicola.

Shimlara, Mully, and Georgio rushed together for a family hug.

"I kept thinking of how frightened you must have been when you got home and found the house deserted and that half-written note from your father," said Mully, her face buried in Shimlara's curly hair.

"I was fine," Shimlara reassured her. "I got right on the phone with the Space Brigade."

"Blanket?" asked Squid hopefully.

"Oh yes, I forgot!" Shimlara pulled the dirty blue square from her pocket. Squid grabbed it and hugged it rapturously.

"Well, as much as I enjoyed the company, I'm very happy to be out of that cell," said the familiar gray-haired lady, stretching her arms over her head.

"Me too," said another tall, thin, gray-haired woman. Nicola noted with interest that her skin was deep green: the exact same color as a well-watered front lawn.

"We've been lucky enough to meet some quite distinguished people during our stay here," said Georgio to

Nicola, as if he'd been at a cocktail party, not a prison camp. "May I present the *United Aunts*!"

Nicola realized that the other prisoners who had shared the Gorgioskio cell were all gray-haired, gracious, intelligent-looking women. Judging by their varying shapes, sizes, and skin colors, they were all from different planets. This was confirmed when each stepped forward, bowed her head, and said the name of the planet she was representing.

Nicola didn't recognize most of the planet names. (For example, the woman with green skin said she was representing the planet of Clock.) However, there were a few that she did recognize. An extremely tall woman with a noticeably large nose said she represented the planet of Globagaskar. A beautiful woman carrying a flute, with long gray hair that nearly touched the ground, said she represented the planet of Whimsy. A gray-haired, scaly-skinned woman said, "I'm somewhat ashamed to say I represent the planet of Volcomania."

Next was the short, fuzzy-haired lady. She smiled at Nicola. "I think you may know my planet. I represent Shobble."

Of course! A Shobbling!

"My planet is a different place thanks to the Space Brigade," said the aunt. All the other aunts looked impressed and Nicola blushed.

Then a slight woman with cropped gray hair stepped out from behind Georgio.

Nicola gasped. "I think you may know my planet, too," said the woman briskly.

Nicola was trying to speak, but no words were coming out of her mouth. She had never been so surprised to see someone in her entire life.

"As you probably guessed," said Nicola's crazy great-aunt Annie, "I represent Earth."

31

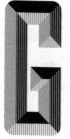**REAT-AUNT ANNIE?" NICOLA FINALLY MANAGED**
to speak.

Sean was back in the Food Hall helping to tie
up the sleeping guards. She wished he were here
to share her shock at this unexpected surprise.

"Those dreadful Volcomanians kidnapped me from
your great-grandmother's birthday party just a few minutes
after you left," said Great-Aunt Annie.

"*You're* one of the United Aunts?" stammered Nicola.

"What's so surprising about that?" said Great-Aunt
Annie.

*Well, for one thing, Dad says you're a nut! Isn't it a
bit embarrassing for Earth to have Great-Aunt Annie as a
representative?*

"Most Earthlings don't even believe in the existence of
life on other planets," said Nicola out loud. "I wouldn't have
thought Earth would have a representative."

"That's why there weren't many applicants for the
position," admitted Great-Aunt Annie. "There was an
advertisement in my local paper about ten years ago. I
think *most people* thought it was a joke, but I thought, *why*

not? They wanted an adventurous aunt with a strong sense of morality who was committed to achieving intergalactic peace. I met all the criteria! I remember I tried to tell the family when I got the position but everyone just thought I'd lost my marbles. So nowadays I pretend to be as clueless about intergalactic life as ordinary Earthlings. That's why when Shimlara called for you at Grammy's party, I put on a little act. I don't know why I bother. You all still think I'm quite crazy!"

"Oh, no we don't," said Nicola unconvincingly.

"Do you think we should postpone all these family reunions for another time?" said a rather cranky-looking aunt from the planet of Doom. "There *is* a war going on."

"You're right," said Mully. She stopped patting Shimlara's hair and she straightened her shoulders and lifted her chin. "What's your strategy, Nicola?"

Nicola was always amazed at the way Shimlara's mother could be transformed from ordinary mom to experienced soldier and back again in a matter of seconds.

"We put rose petals in the guards' food to make them sleep," she said. "We're tying them up at the moment. Then we'll—anyway, I'll explain the rest later." She was suddenly worried that Mully would think their strategy was dumb.

"Sounds like you're doing a great job," said Mully encouragingly.

"I do hope you're not going against the United Aunts' 'Play Nice' Guidelines," said the plump aunt who represented the planet of Plenty. "The United Aunts do not condone nastiness."

"Er—we're tying them up as nicely as possible," said Nicola.

When they got back to the hall, they found Tyler and Katie tying the last of the guards to chairs.

"The prisoners were *very* enthusiastic about helping," said Sean to Nicola. His eyes widened. *"Great-Aunt Annie?"*

"Is that my president *tied to a chair*?" said the aunt who represented Volcomania. She pointed at Mrs. Mania, who was still sleeping in spite of the ropes tying her to the chair. "When she wakes up, she is going to be *furious*!"

"I don't care if she's furious." Nicola marched up to Mrs. Mania's chair. She bent down and checked the ropes to make sure Mrs. Mania had no hope of escaping.

"Nicola," said Katie.

"What?" Nicola was busy giving the rope around Mrs. Mania's ankle an extra-firm tug.

"Nicola," said Katie again.

Nicola looked up and froze.

Mrs. Mania's nose twitched. She moved her mouth around as if it were full of marbles. She opened her eyes and looked around blearily, taking in the sight of her tied-up son, the tied-up guards, and the released prisoners staring back at her.

Finally her eyes fell on Nicola, still crouched down beside her, and her scaly skin turned a purplish red, as if she'd been placed in a vat of boiling water.

"Who are you and what is going on here?"

32

 **ICOLA HAD NEVER SEEN ANYONE SO ANGRY IN** her entire life. She backed quickly away from Mrs. Mania's chair and joined the others, her eyes fixed on the furious president.

"I think her head is about to explode," said Sean with interest.

"She doesn't have any control over her emotions," commented Great-Aunt Annie disapprovingly.

"You might find it useful to take a few deep breaths and count to ten!" called out Georgio.

Mrs. Mania's eyes flashed fire. She snarled like a wild animal. Her chair skidded across the raised platform as she tried to escape from the ropes, jerking her body this way and that as though she were trying to win some kind of demented dancing competition.

"Told you we needed to tie her up good and tight," said one of the Volcomanian prisoners with satisfaction.

"Whoever is responsible for this will pay the price!" screamed Mrs. Mania.

Everyone instinctively took a step backward.

"Perhaps we should surrender now?" murmured Henry.

"Don't be silly," said Nicola, trying to sound braver than she felt. "You must never give in to bullies."

"Really?" said Henry. "Why not?"

Nicola marched up to Mrs. Mania, clenching her teeth hard to stop her head from wobbling with fright. (It wobbled when she was nervous.)

Whenever I feel intimidated by someone, I try to imagine what they were like as a baby, Nicola's mother had once told her.

Nicola tried to imagine Mrs. Mania as a red-faced baby kicking her legs and banging her fists in a high chair, but actually, she still seemed scary, even as a baby.

Or if that doesn't work, I pretend I'm an Academy Award–winning actress playing the role of a courageous heroine, Nicola's mother had continued.

Nicola imagined herself on a big movie screen wearing a shiny black leather outfit and striding across a battlefield. *Mmmm, that's better.*

"Mrs. Mania," she began. "My name is Nicola Berry and I—"

"*I know who you are! You're nothing more than an Earthling child!*"

Nicola's ears rang. "My age isn't relevant—"

"*You're playing with fire this time, girlie, and you're going to get hurt!*"

"Please don't call me girlie," said Nicola. She couldn't stand that word.

"Stay out of this war and get back on your own piddling planet!"

Nicola decided not to say anything else. She just crossed her arms and stared at Mrs. Mania, her eyebrows raised in a superior fashion. After all, Mrs. Mania was the one tied to a chair.

It seemed to work.

Mrs. Mania stared back at her for a while, grinding her teeth like a tiger about to pounce. Finally she snarled, "What do you want?"

"We'd like you to order the withdrawal of your troops from this planet," said Nicola, knowing full well that wasn't going to happen.

"That isn't going to happen!"

"Yes." Nicola winced with her hands over her ears. "I thought not."

"Mom?" said a voice.

Mrs. Mania's pale, plump son, who looked about the same age as Nicola and the others, had opened his eyes and was looking around in amazement.

"How did I get tied up like this?" he said. "The last thing I remember is taking a bite of yummy sausage. I was looking forward to my next bite."

Mrs. Mania's voice and manner changed completely. It was obvious she absolutely adored her son.

"Don't be frightened, Martykins," she said. "This silly Earthling is sticking her nose into matters that don't concern her."

"Mom," said Marty, looking mortified. "Please don't call me Martykins in public." He looked around him worriedly. "Where is Princess Petronella?"

Princess Petronella lifted a languid hand from where she was sitting. "I'm over here, Marty!"

"Hi, Princess! Hi! How are you? Are you okay?" Marty's face turned pink with pleasure. It was obvious that he had something of a crush on the princess.

"So much for diplomatic visits! It looks like your friend is in cahoots with the enemy, Martyki—I mean, Martin," said Mrs. Mania. "We may have to declare war on Globa-gaskar next."

The United Aunts stepped forward as one and shook their fingers. "We strongly object to angry declarations of war," they chanted firmly. Nicola felt quite proud to see her great-aunt Annie chanting with the other aunts.

Mrs. Mania rolled her eyes and made a huffing sound like a bad-tempered teenager.

"Mom," said Marty. "I think you should show the United Aunts more respect."

"Oh, I do respect them, darling." Mrs. Mania grinned. "That's why I had them kidnapped. I needed them out of the way until we've won this war and Whimsy has surrendered."

"About that," said Nicola. "The people of Whimsy have a message for you."

"They've had enough and they're going to surrender, are they?"

"Not exactly," said Nicola. "May I present Henry Sweet, the president of Whimsy."

Henry stepped forward, nervously pulling off his beret, so a tuft of hair stood up like a peacock. He didn't look at all presidential.

"Not off somewhere painting a pretty picture then, Henry?" said Mrs. Mania.

"Ah, no, not right now," said Henry. He brightened. "Although I was just looking at the specks of dust dancing in the beam of light streaming through that window over there and it gave me a rather marvelous idea—"

Nicola shook her head at him. Henry coughed and cleared his throat.

"The people of Whimsy would like to challenge you to a battle to, um, end all battles." Henry carefully recited the script the Space Brigade had worked out the night before. "If you win the battle, we shall surrender. If we win the

battle, you shall formally recognize Whimsy as an independent planet and immediately withdraw your troops and
promise to never, ever declare war upon us again."

"You're kidding, right?" said Mrs. Mania.

"Ah, no," said Henry. "I'm perfectly serious. We propose
the battle takes place at the Sublime Valley at sunset today."

"You actually think you have a chance of defeating the
finest army in the galaxy! Whimsy doesn't even have an
army!"

"I wouldn't say we were exactly full of *confidence*,"
admitted Henry.

Mrs. Mania laughed out loud. She shook her head almost
fondly at Henry. "This is exactly why you can't rule yourselves! You have no grip on reality."

"It's funny you should mention that," said Henry. "I was
just thinking to myself, *Could all this be a terrible dream?*
And yet it feels so real!"

Mrs. Mania rolled her eyes. "I suppose the Space Brigade
is behind this idea of yours?" She shot Nicola a malevolent
look.

"Umm, well—" Henry blushed. (The people of Whimsy
were terrible blushers.)

"What if we are?" spoke up Nicola. "Are you frightened
of us?"

Excellent, Nicola! Georgio's voice suddenly rang out

clearly in Nicola's head. *Now watch her snap up the bait like a hungry fish!*

He was right. Mrs. Mania bristled.

"Frightened of *Earthling children*?" she cried. "Your challenge is accepted, Henry Sweet! *Prepare to be annihilated!*"

33

OVELY," SAID HENRY SWEET, BEFORE REALIZING that probably wasn't the most appropriate response to *"Prepare to be annihilated!"* and being overcome with embarrassment. "I mean, er, well, let's see now—"

Nicola interrupted him.

"You might be thinking that even if you lose, you can always back out of this deal," she said to Mrs. Mania.

"That's *exactly* what she's thinking," spoke up Shimlara, who had obviously been reading Mrs. Mania's mind.

"Fortunately, we've got insurance," said Nicola.

"Insurance?" Mrs. Mania frowned.

Tyler stepped forward carrying his video camera. "I filmed the whole thing," he said.

"If you lose the battle and go back on your word," said Nicola, "we will broadcast this footage to the entire galaxy."

"You're not real journalists!" said Mrs. Mania.

"No, but this *is* a real camera," said Nicola, thinking that it was lucky that Mrs. Mania couldn't read minds, or she might have discovered that Tyler's camera had actually been ruined by the policewomen's water hoses during the protest.

"I think the intergalactic community would be very interested to hear how you've treated the United Aunts," said the green-skinned aunt.

"Every planet in the galaxy would be furious with you," said the aunt representing the planet of Shobble. "I would certainly be recommending that my planet didn't export any more ShobbleChoc to you!"

Marty Mania's mouth dropped in horror. "Mom! Don't let that happen! I couldn't live without ShobbleChoc!"

"Don't worry, Marty," said Mrs. Mania testily. "We're not going to lose the battle."

"What battle?" said a rough voice.

"Yes, what battle?"

The sleeping Volcomanian guards were waking up. (They must have taken much bigger first mouthfuls of their food than Mrs. Mania and her son, so they'd slept for longer.)

As the guards realized they were tied to their chairs and struggled to free themselves, there was a terrible din.

"Who tied me up?"

"I only had one mouthful of my breakfast and now it looks like it's gone cold!"

"QUIET!"

It was Mrs. Mania. (Her voice projection was quite outstanding.)

The guards fell silent.

"Not another word," she said. "I blame every single one of you for the indignity I have suffered today. So I suggest you zip your lips and consider new careers because *you're all fired*!"

"But—" began the guard who had reminded Nicola and Sean of the school bully.

"Zip it!" shouted Mrs. Mania.

She looked at Nicola. "I assume you'll be untying me and my son now? I don't mind if you want to leave these incompetent guards but obviously someone of my position should not be expected to feel this level of discomfort."

"Ah, no," said Nicola. "Call us crazy, but we don't actually trust you."

"And just how am I meant to contact my troops?" asked Mrs. Mania. "I need my hands free to control my radio." She jerked her chin at the large radio sitting on the table next to her breakfast plate.

"That's no problem," said Sean confidently. "I can operate it."

He went striding up to the platform and bent over the radio, studying the controls. "Easy," he said, and twiddled a few knobs. "There you go." He held the radio microphone up to her lips.

Mrs. Mania grimaced. Then she shrugged and began to speak.

"Come in all platoons, all platoons come in. This is Mrs. Mania. Good news! The Whimsians have challenged us to a battle in the Sublime Valley tonight at sunset. Once you've all stopped laughing, please proceed to the valley. It should be a quick, easy battle that will wrap up this war once and for all. Expect to be back with your families in time for dinner."

The radio crackled as the deep-voiced captains in charge of each Volcomanian platoon responded.

"Copy that, looking forward to it, Madam!"

"Should be amusing, Madam!"

"It will be like defeating a litter of kittens!"

After each captain had responded and Sean turned off the radio, Mrs. Mania grinned nastily at Nicola and Henry Sweet.

"Are you sure you don't want to forget the whole thing?"

"Maybe we should," said Henry to Nicola, his eyes wide with alarm.

"Of course we shouldn't!" said Nicola. "We'll leave you here for now, Mrs. Mania, but we'll be back to collect you at sunset so you can watch the battle for yourself."

"And me too?" asked her son eagerly.

"You too," said Nicola. She felt rather sorry for Marty Mania. "Come on, everybody. It's time for our breakfast."

The Space Brigade, the prisoners, the United Aunts,

and the Gorgioskio family left the food hall together. The piggy eyes of the guards silently watched them go.

"I really think someone should stay and keep an eye on those guards," said Greta.

"Everyone is hungry," said Nicola snappishly. She was sick of Greta thinking she knew best. "They've all been tied up securely. Nobody is going to escape."

As arranged, Poppy the waitress had left a huge picnic outside the prison gates.

The Space Brigade and Henry Sweet stood back politely and waited while the starving prisoners fell upon the food. It was wonderful to see the color coming back into their cheeks, and the light returning to their eyes as they ate and drank.

"There is something familiar about that aunt with the fuzzy gray hair," said Katie quietly to Nicola, pointing at the picnic rug where the United Aunts were sitting with very straight backs tucking into sausage sandwiches.

"That's because she represents the planet of Shobble," explained Nicola. Most of the people of the planet of Shobble shared similar features: fuzzy hair and round, sweet faces.

"A Shobbling!" said Sean. "We can ask her, then!"

"Ask her what?"

"Ask her what the limited edition gold buttons do," said Sean.

He walked over to the picnic blanket where the aunts were sitting. They watched him bend down and show the Shobbling aunt the button around his neck.

A few minutes later he was back with a big grin on his face.

"So?" said Nicola.

"It lets you unbutton your mistakes," he said.

"What do you mean?"

"She said if you make a mistake that you can't fix any other way, you just hold the button between your fingertips and say, *'Let that moment retake, so I can unbutton my mistake.'* You'll get a second chance to fix things. Nobody else except you will ever remember you made the mistake."

"Gosh." Katie carefully held up her button and looked at it with awe.

"I bet it doesn't work," said Greta. "It seems very unlikely to me."

"I wonder what technology it uses," said Tyler.

"Well, I'm *always* making mistakes," said Shimlara. "It should come in very handy."

"That's the other thing," said Sean. "She said you can only use it once. That's why it's called a limited edition. She said to make sure you only use it for a really *serious* mistake."

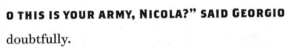

34

SO THIS IS YOUR ARMY, NICOLA?" SAID GEORGIO doubtfully.

It was later that afternoon. Nicola looked at the huge crowd of Whimsians gathered in front of the prison camp. They had all responded to Henry Sweet's "Call to Arms" the night before. Not surprisingly, there was no electronic means of communication on Whimsy. Instead, messages were sent on miniature scrolls of parchment, carried by white doves in their beaks.

"At least everyone seems very *busy*," said one of the United Aunts.

This was true. Artists feverishly painted huge canvases. Sculptors were up to their elbows in wet clay.

"They might not look like an army—" said Nicola to Georgio.

"You've got that right!"

Before Nicola could say any more, Henry Sweet hurried up to her, wringing his hands. "The artists are arguing over color schemes. This is unexpectedly stressful. I might need to lie down."

"You can lie down once we've won the war, Henry," said

Nicola. She looked up at the sky. Whimsy's giant sun had begun to slide toward the horizon. "We haven't got long before sunset."

"Maybe you could take us through your strategy one more time, Nicola?" said Georgio.

"She doesn't have time," said Mully. "We're going to have to trust the Space Brigade. They've proven themselves before. I think their plan is very . . . creative."

"That's one word for it," said Georgio grimly.

"Do you have any other ideas, Dad?" asked Shimlara impatiently.

"Not exactly," admitted Georgio.

"Then instead of complaining, maybe you could be asking how you could help!"

"Putting aside your rather undaughterly tone, you make a good point," said Georgio. He turned to Nicola. "How can we help?"

"Everyone has been assigned to a platoon," said Nicola. "So I suggest you report to your platoon leader and await orders."

"Aye, aye, sir!" Georgio saluted Nicola as if she were a ship's admiral. "Who is my platoon captain?"

Shimlara smiled. "That would be me, Dad."

"Excellent. I'll feel right at home being bossed around by my daughter."

Squid removed his thumb from his mouth. "I want to be on your plate, too!" he cried, looking up imploringly at his big sister.

"Don't worry, you're in my platoon, too," said Shimlara. She hoisted Squid up onto her hip.

"What about me?" asked Mully. "Am I in Shimlara's platoon, too?"

"Actually, seeing as you're the only person with actual army experience, you have your own platoon," said Nicola. She hoped that Georgio wouldn't be upset about his wife being a platoon captain, when he was a lowly soldier, but she needn't have worried.

"Mully's platoon will put the others to shame!" he said with satisfaction.

"Thanks a lot, Dad," said Shimlara. "Great team spirit."

"What? Oh! Sorry, darling, I mean, oh dear, I do put my heel in my mouth sometimes."

"Foot in your mouth," corrected Greta under her breath.

"What's she mumbling about?" said Georgio irritably.

"The United Aunts are all in Mully's platoon." Nicola squinted at the piece of paper she'd been scribbling on last night.

"Right," said Mully. "And what's our objective?"

"Your objective is to infiltrate the enemy lines and to sabotage their tanks," said Nicola, wondering if this was actually possible for a group of elderly aunts. "If that's okay?"

"No problem," said Mully, as if Nicola had just asked her to pass the milk.

"What's our objective?" Georgio asked Shimlara respectfully.

"Intelligence," said Shimlara. "We have to read the enemy's minds and report anything useful to Nicola. We'll be scanning thousands of soldiers' minds all at the same time."

Princess Petronella sauntered over to Nicola.

"I hear that you're assigning people to platoons," she said. "I assume I'll be commander in chief of a battalion, perhaps?"

It hadn't actually occurred to Nicola to give the princess a specific role.

"Ah, we thought of you as more of a . . . figurehead," she said.

"Figurehead." The princess frowned. "That must be an Earthling word. I expect it means *Queen of Everything*?"

"Sort of," said Nicola. No need to mention that figureheads didn't actually have any authority.

"Excellent," said the princess. "I'll go and check on everybody's progress."

"Thanks," said Nicola. She turned back to her list and checked off the roles for everyone else.

Sean—Captain of the Theatrical Platoon

Katie—Captain of the Music Platoon

Tyler—Captain of the Sculptors Platoon

Henry Sweet—Captain of the Painters Platoon

Greta—Captain of the Writers and Poets Platoon

Nicola—GENERAL

Nicola looked around her to check on how all the other platoon captains were doing.

Sean was trying to make his platoon do push-ups without much success. There was a lot of theatrical groaning and collapsing.

To Nicola's surprise, Katie was speaking extremely sternly to her music platoon. "We're going to practice again," she said. "Again and *again*. Until we get it perfect."

Tyler's sculptors were working hard, as were Henry's painters. Meanwhile, Greta's writers and poets seemed to be . . . crying. *Oh dear.*

Nicola hurried over to see what was going on.

"I don't know what's wrong with them," snapped Greta when she saw Nicola approach.

"She said my beautiful words were 'garbage,'" sobbed one of the poets.

"I don't think writers handle criticism very well," said Nicola quietly to Greta. "You need to be more encouraging."

She turned to Greta's platoon.

"You are the best and most talented writers and poets in the galaxy!" she told them. "You write exquisitely! Your words can help win this war! Please, do not give up! We need you!"

The writers and poets sniffed, wiped their eyes, picked up their pencils, and got back to work.

"Thank you, Nicola," said Greta sincerely. "That was very helpful of you."

Nicola was a bit thrown by Greta's uncharacteristic gratitude but she didn't have time to think about it because at that moment she heard a sound like the beating of a drum in the distance. "What's that?"

One of the Whimsian writers looked up from his notebook.

"It's the sound of marching boots," he said. "The Volcomanian army must be close."

Nicola looked up at the sky and saw that Whimsy's giant sun had sunk even lower in the sky.

Icy fingers of fear caressed her neck.

The battle was about to begin.

35

T WAS SUNSET ON THE PLANET OF WHIMSY. THE sky was the color of crushed strawberries.

Or the color of blood.

Nicola shivered.

"Are you chilly?" said Princess Petronella.

"I'm fine." Nicola lowered her binoculars.

She and the princess were standing on a small, rocky outcrop on the side of a mountain above the Sublime Valley. It was a perfect vantage spot to observe the army below.

The Volcomanian tanks had rolled into the valley just before sunset, along with what seemed like thousands of soldiers marching in straight-backed, stiff-armed formation. Their boots and buttons shone. Their weapons were slung over their shoulders at the same angle. This was an army that knew exactly what it was doing.

Nicola held her portable radio provided by XYZ40 close to her mouth.

"Come in, Shimlara," she said, feeling self-conscious. "Over."

Shimlara, Georgio, and Squid had a hiding spot lower

down the mountain, where they were close enough to see the soldiers' faces so they could read their minds.

Shimlara's voice came over the radio. "This is Shimlara."

"Have you—"

"Over!"

"Beg your pardon?" said Nicola.

"I forgot to say *over* after I said 'This is Shimlara.' Over."

"Oh, okay. What have you got to report?" She paused. "Shimlara?"

"Sorry, I was waiting for you to say over! Over."

Princess Petronella snickered.

"Have you read the minds of any of the Volcomanian soldiers?" asked Nicola. "What are they thinking? Over."

"They're all very relaxed. Most of them seem to think that we've chickened out," said Shimlara. "Dad says he's never read more smug minds. Oh, and Squid wanted me to tell you that a soldier called Pete is looking forward to a fried armchair for his dinner. I think his reading might be a bit off. Over."

"Thanks, Shimlara," said Nicola. "Over and out."

She turned to look at the princess. "It's time to attack."

"You have my approval," said Princess Petronella grandly.

Nicola hid a smile and picked up her radio. "Come in Sean, Katie, Greta, Tyler, and Henry!"

The other platoon captains were all scattered at different points overlooking the valley. Everyone except for Henry answered immediately.

"Henry?" said Nicola.

"Sorry!" said Henry after a second. "I was overcome by the eerie sensation of hearing your voice through this remarkable machine."

"I want you to attack on the count of three," said Nicola into the radio.

"Four," interrupted Princess Petronella. "Nobody ever does anything important on the count of three. You do it on the count of four."

"On Earth we—" began Nicola. "Oh, forget it. Fine." She clicked the button on the radio again. "On the count of four, I want you to attack. One . . ."

"Four?" Greta's cranky voice spoke through the radio. "Don't you mean three?"

Henry spoke up. "On the planet of Whimsy we do things on the count of twenty-two. It's such a pleasing number."

Oh for heaven's sake.

"Attack!" cried Nicola. *"Attack now!"*

36

**ICOLA HELD HER BREATH. THIS COULD BE** highly embarrassing if it didn't work.

"Nothing is happening," said Princess Petronella.

"Wait. Listen."

First there was a sound like galloping hooves.

"Horses?" said the princess. "Where did you get horses from?"

"It's not horses," said Nicola. "It's Katie's musical platoon. It's actually drums."

"No, they're real! Look! It's a whole army!"

Thousands of soldiers on horseback were galloping over the ridge of the mountains toward the valley below. The soldiers wore scarlet coats over white pants. They carried bayonets that caught the light. The horses were fine-looking creatures with black shiny coats. It was an amazing and terrifying scene. Blood-curdling cries rang out across the mountain.

"Chaa-aaarge!"

"We will never surrender until we beat the offender!"

"There is nothing flimsy about the soldiers of Whimsy!"

"Where did you get a real army from?" marveled the princess.

"It's not real," said Nicola, although she could hardly believe it wasn't real herself. "That's a painting by Henry Sweet's platoon. They've got a huge canvas up there and they're shaking it to make it look like they're moving."

"But they're real voices!"

"They're actors," said Nicola. "It's Sean's theatrical platoon. They're reading a script by Greta's writers and poets. This is a show. A huge show by the people of Whimsy."

Nicola picked up the radio again. "Shimlara? Are they falling for it?"

Shimlara answered immediately.

"They're in shock! Most of their minds are completely blank! Dad said one of the platoon captains just thought to himself, *We're in trouble.*"

"You can't tell me that enormous tank isn't real!" said the princess in disbelief.

A massive black tank appeared on the crest of the mountain. It was about twenty times the size of the Volcomanian tanks and seemed to black out half the sky.

"It's a sculpture," said Nicola. "Tyler designed it and the Whimsy sculptors built it."

The tank fired. The sound was deafening. The sky was illuminated with shooting flames and clouds of smoke.

"Sound effects and fireworks!" yelled Nicola over the noise to the princess.

"I approve!" cried the princess, jumping with joy. "As your figurehead, I approve!"

Shimlara's gleeful voice came over the radio. "Half the soldiers are thinking about surrendering. The other half want their mothers."

Nicola took up her binoculars.

Some of the Volcomanian soldiers had dropped their weapons and were running for cover. Others were running to their own tanks.

Oh dear.

Nicola quickly picked up the radio. "Come in, Mully. Mully, come in."

Mully answered immediately, her voice clear and crisp. "This is Mully, Nicola. The United Aunts and I are behind enemy lines and we have successfully achieved our mission objective. Over."

"You mean their tanks won't work?"

"Correct. Over."

"Wow! That's amazing! How did you do that?"

Mully's voice changed back to her ordinary mom voice. "Maybe I could tell you that later, honey, once we've actually won the battle?"

"Oh yes, of course! Thanks, Mully! Over and out."

Nicola picked up her binoculars. She could see the Volcomanians slamming frustrated fists against the sides of the tanks.

Shimlara's voice came over the radio.

"They're freaking out! They don't know what to do!"

Her voice changed abruptly. "Bad news! Dad just read the mind of one of the Volcomanian captains. He's starting to suspect it's a trick. He's noticed the soldiers on horseback aren't getting closer."

Nicola felt a shot of adrenaline. It was time for their final move.

"Come in, Sean," she said.

"Yeah, Nic?"

"We need Mrs. Mania right now."

"Gotcha."

Nicola hung up the radio and bit her lip.

Shimlara's voice came over the radio again, filled with trepidation. "Nicola! The suspicious captain is about to order his men to charge up the mountain!"

At that moment, a familiar voice rang out across the valley.

"Soldiers of Volcomania! This is Mrs. Mania, your commander in chief! I order you to lay down your weapons!"

"Why is she saying that?" asked the princess.

"It's not really Mrs. Mania. It's Poppy the waitress,"

explained Nicola. "She's an actress. Of course, we had to make it look like they were losing the battle first before we used her. Otherwise it would have looked too suspicious."

"She sounds exactly like her," said the princess. "I approve!"

Shimlara's voice crackled over the radio again. "They're falling for it!"

Nicola looked through the binoculars and saw the soldiers carefully placing their weapons on the ground with confused expressions on their faces.

"Now put your fists in your armpits and flap your arms like chickens!"

That was obviously Sean's idea. Was it going too far?

Nicola grinned as she saw the Volcomanian soldiers obediently flapping their arms.

"Now say cluck cluck—"

"STOP RIGHT THERE!"

Another voice boomed across the valley.

Nicola clapped her hand to her mouth.

"Have you got *two* actresses playing Mrs. Mania?" asked Princess Petronella.

"No," said Nicola frantically. "That's the *real* Mrs. Mania!"

Mrs. Mania and her son had been taken to observe the battle from a convenient tower overlooking the valley (normally used as a poet's retreat) under the guard of the released prisoners. How had she escaped? There had been at least fifty prisoners keeping watch over her!

Nicola's radio crackled with worried cries from the other members of the Space Brigade.

"What's going on, Nicola?"

"Is that the real Mrs. Mania?"

"Should the fake Mrs. Mania keep talking?"

"YOU HAVE BEEN DECEIVED BY SMOKE AND MIRRORS, YOU FOOLS! THERE IS NO WHIMSIAN ARMY!"

"Mrs. Mania is free!" said Princess Petronella.

She pointed over Nicola's shoulder.

Mrs. Mania was marching down the mountain path from the Lookout Tower in her stiletto heels, a huge megaphone in her hand. Nicola lifted her binoculars and adjusted them to focus on Mrs. Mania's face. She was smiling triumphantly. Her son, Marty Mania, walked alongside her, looking mortified.

A group of familiar-looking people stomped behind Mrs. Mania and her son. *The guards from the prison camp!* They must have overcome the prisoners. But how had they escaped from the food hall?

I shouldn't have left the food hall unguarded, thought Nicola. *That was a mistake. A stupid mistake! I just didn't want to take Greta's advice.*

Mrs. Mania lifted her megaphone again.

"PICK THOSE WEAPONS BACK UP!"

"As your figurehead," said Princess Petronella to Nicola, "I have to tell you that I don't approve of this at all."

"CHARGE!"

37

**ICOLA TURNED AWAY FROM MRS. MANIA AND** looked through the binoculars at the Volcomanian soldiers below. They were charging up the mountain like wounded bulls, weapons held high, their scaly-skinned faces red with rage and humiliation.

"Should we surrender?" Henry's trembling voice came over the radio. "I think we should surrender!"

We were so, so close! If it weren't for my stupid mistake—

Mistake.

Nicola's hand flew to her neck, where she kept her limited edition gold button. What did Sean say? *To unbutton your mistake, just hold the button between your fingertips and say . . .*

Nicola put the button between her fingertips and said out loud, "Let that moment retake, so I can unbutton my mistake."

The world went black.

The air rushed from her lungs. She was flying backward through something like a long railway tunnel. There was a thin shrieking sound in her ears and a strange smell like the burning of rubber in her nostrils.

Oh my goodness! Is this SAFE?

"Nicola?"

Nicola blinked. She was standing outside the food hall with the released prisoners, the Space Brigade, and Henry Sweet. Greta was looking at Nicola expectantly.

"I *said*, should we leave someone to guard the food hall?" Nicola couldn't believe it. It was earlier that same day. She'd actually traveled backward in time! This was her chance to fix the mistake and make everything right!

She threw her arms around Greta.

"*Yes!* That's a *fantastic* idea!"

Greta looked appalled by Nicola's sudden burst of affection. "Okay, okay."

"And I think someone should check all the guards' pockets," added Nicola. "One of the guards might have a pocket knife. It would be disastrous if they escaped."

"Good idea," said Sean. "We'll do it now." He went back into the food hall with a few of the other prisoners. A few moments later he came back out holding a penknife.

"That bully of a guard had it in his back pocket!" he said. "I bet he might have been able to get one of his meaty hands to it and cut himself free! What made you think of it?"

"You'll never guess—"

Before she had a chance to explain, the world went black and Nicola was flying again. Only this time she was flying forward with that same shrieking sound and burning smell.

"Nicola?"

Nicola gasped, her head spinning. She was back on the mountain again standing next to Princess Petronella. She put her hand to her neck. Her limited edition gold button was gone.

"What's the matter?" said Princess Petronella. "Your face has gone a strange color."

Nicola looked over her shoulder and up at the Lookout Tower.

"Is she free?"

"Who?"

"The real Mrs. Mania?"

"I don't think so," said the princess. "Should she be? I wouldn't approve of that. Isn't she safely tied up in the tower? Oh, look, they're still clucking like chickens! Mrs. Mania must be writhing in agony!"

Nicola lifted her binoculars and watched the army below clucking like chickens. For a moment she was confused, and then her mind cleared. It had worked! She'd traveled back through time, fixed her mistake, and made everything right again! And best of all, she'd done it on her own: calmly, quickly, efficiently. Princess Petronella obviously had no memory of Mrs. Mania escaping. It was just like it had never happened. Nobody even had to know she'd ever made that mistake.

Nicola's horrendous feeling of guilt vanished and the relief was blissful. She wanted to run around in circles, punching both fists in the air like a soccer player who had just scored the winning goal. She touched the empty spot around her neck where the limited edition gold button had hung. What an incredible, wondrous piece of technology. She would have to send the people of Shobble the most grateful thank-you note she had ever written.

The fake Mrs. Mania's voiced boomed out across the valley. Poppy was doing an excellent job.

"Now form a conga line and dance up the mountain toward the Lookout Tower!"

Nicola watched in amazement as the soldiers formed a conga line with their hands on one another's waists.

She picked up the radio. "Shimlara? What are the soldiers thinking?"

"They think Mrs. Mania has finally lost her mind," answered Shimlara. "But they're all happy the war is over. None of them really believed in it, anyway. They all secretly liked the planet of Whimsy."

Katie's musical platoon struck up a tune, and the

Volcomanian army began to dance up the mountain, kicking their legs and swinging their hips in perfect time to the music.

"They're quite good dancers," remarked Princess Petronella.

Nicola picked up the radio again. "Everyone report to the Lookout Tower to watch Mrs. Mania squirm! It looks like Whimsy has won the war!"

There were excited cries from the Space Brigade and a strange sound that Nicola was pretty sure was Henry Sweet bursting into tears.

She and the princess hurried up the path toward the tower. Night was beginning to fall, and Whimsy's jewelry box of stars was slowly emerging in the sky.

She and the princess reached the tower and hurried up a circular staircase to where Mrs. Mania and Marty Mania were sitting, still tied to their chairs, looking out the window at the conga line of soldiers snaking its way up the mountain in the starlight. The released prisoners who had been guarding Mrs. Mania were cheering as if they were at a football game.

Nicola had expected Mrs. Mania's face to be red with rage, but instead it was dead white, as if she were seriously ill.

"You call this *winning a battle*?" she spat out, when she

saw Nicola. "I've never seen anything more disgusting or deceitful!"

"Oh, but bombing a *preschool* is okay?" said Nicola.

"This is making a mockery of war! You had some foolish little actress pretending to be me! That's against the law! And now you've got my soldiers *dancing*! That's so disrespectful!"

"Your soldiers seem to be enjoying it," pointed out Princess Petronella.

"And as for you, young lady." Mrs. Mania thrust an angry finger at Princess Petronella. "What disgusting behavior for a guest! I shall be writing to the king and queen of Globagaskar."

"Why don't you?" said the princess airily. "My parents will be proud of me!"

"Anyway," said Nicola. "I assume you will now honor your commitment and withdraw your troops."

"Never!" screamed Mrs. Mania.

"I beg your pardon?" said Nicola. "But we won!"

At that moment the rest of the Space Brigade, Henry Sweet, Mully, Georgio, and the now rather disheveled-looking United Aunts came into the room, all of them flushed with victory and slapping one another on the back.

"I don't care if you won or not! I shall fight this war until

the day I die!" roared Mrs. Mania. She bounced around so much on her chair that it nearly toppled over.

There was silence for a few seconds as everyone in the room stared at the strange, demented woman.

The United Aunts sighed, folded their arms across their chests, and shook their heads disappointedly.

"That's it, I know the United Aunts disapprove of violence but I'm giving her a good rap across the knuckles with my wooden spoon," said the green-skinned United Aunt.

"If I were to paint this woman," said Henry, "I would give her the head of a viper."

"I'm so sick of her! Let's just throw her out of the tower window!" said a Volcomanian war protester who had been imprisoned in the camp, and was obviously still not very happy about it.

The room erupted as everyone argued over the best thing to do next.

And then the only person in the room with any power over Mrs. Mania spoke up.

38

OTHER," SAID MARTY MANIA.

He spoke quietly and forcefully. His soft, plump face became hard. He seemed twenty years older.

"That is enough. You are embarrassing me. You are embarrassing the planet of Volcomania."

"Marty, you don't understand." Mrs. Mania squirmed in her chair.

"No, Mother, I don't! I never understood the point of this war, anyway! What has Whimsy ever done to us?"

"It's simple geography! Whimsy is not its own planet. It's a *suburb* of Volcomania. Why should they get all this beauty to themselves? Look at all that fertile soil out there!" Mrs. Mania jerked her head out the window at the velvet-green soil. "They don't do anything with it, except lie around making up their pathetic poems. Then they come whining to us when they run out of food. We could farm that land! We would make something of this place. If we had Whimsy, Volcomania would be the most successful planet in the galaxy! Don't you see, Marty, I'm doing this for Volcomania!"

"But it's not what the Whimsian people want!" said Marty.

"Who cares about them?! They're annoying! So impractical, so . . . *whimsical*."

"I think we should work *with* the Whimsian people," said Marty. "I have some ideas about how we could help them and they could help us."

Henry Sweet nodded at Marty. "I'd like to hear those ideas, young man!"

"Well, my dear son, if you were in charge of Volcomania then you could be as chummy as you wanted with Mr. Sweet," said Mrs. Mania. "However—"

"That's the thing, Mother," said Marty. "I was talking to one of the United Aunts, the one representing Earth."

Nicola's great-aunt Annie gave a cheery wiggle of her fingers.

"And she said that according to the *United Aunts Intergalactic Convention for Sensible Governance of Planets*, if a planet's leader is seen to act in a way that is deemed to be foolish, bad-mannered, or violent, then a close family member may apply to the United Aunts to automatically take over the leadership."

"What in the world are you telling me this for?" said Mrs. Mania.

"I put in an application to take over the leadership,"

said Marty. "The United Aunts approved it."

Nicola's great-aunt Annie held up an application form with a huge APPROVED stamp across it. Nicola had never been prouder of her aunt.

"So you're no longer president of Volcomania," said Marty. "I am."

"I beg your pardon?" said Mrs. Mania. Her voice had become quite hoarse.

"You heard me, Mother. I'm the new president. And my first act as president will be to honor the commitment you made. We lost the battle. So we will now formally recognize Whimsy as an independent planet, withdraw our troops, and promise never to declare war on Whimsy again. If someone wouldn't mind untying me, I'll make an announcement."

Sean leaped forward to cut the ropes around Marty with the penknife he'd taken from the guard. Marty stood up, stretched, and shook Sean's hand.

"But—I—Marty—this—you—we—how—why . . ." Mrs. Mania's voice drifted away. Her face seemed to collapse inward. A lock of her hair fell in her eyes.

She was a broken woman. Nicola could hardly bear to look at her.

Marty patted his mother on the shoulder. "It's okay, Mom," he said softly. Then he turned to Henry. "Will you join me on the balcony? We can tell our people together that the war is over."

"Certainly," said Henry. "But first, there are some people I need to thank." He turned to the Space Brigade first. "I am overwhelmed with gratitude," he said, solemnly clasping each of their hands in both of his. "The people of Whimsy will never forget. Our children's children will hear songs and stories and poems about the glorious, heroic Space Brigade!"

When he got to Nicola, he shook his head in wonder. "I have learned so much about leadership from you! In the future, whenever I face a difficult problem, I will ask myself, 'What would the president of Earth do?'"

"Nicola isn't the *president of Earth*!" exploded Greta.

"Oh, isn't she? Sorry, I just assumed . . . ," said Henry, while Nicola blushed furiously. "You're just so confident."

Gosh. It was lucky Henry didn't know what was *really* going on inside her head.

Sure is lucky, laughed Shimlara's voice in Nicola's head.

Henry turned to Georgio, Mully, and Squid next.

"Where would we be without people like you! People unafraid to stand up and say, *'This is wrong!'* I'm overcome!"

Tears rolled down Henry's face as he craned his head to look up at Georgio and Mully. Squid, who was the same height as Henry, solemnly patted him on the head.

"It's our pleasure," said Georgio and Mully together.

Next Henry hugged every single one of the United Aunts.

"Ahem," said Marty with meaning. "Maybe we could . . ."

"What? Oh! Yes, of course!"

Henry and Marty stepped out onto the balcony.

A few minutes later there was a tremendous roar of applause. Stunning fireworks lit up Whimsy's night sky in a frenzy of celebratory color. Nicola turned to the other members of the Space Brigade and smiled. "I think our work here is done."

39

CAREFUL!" **KATIE CALLED OUT TO SEAN.**

He was bouncing on his toes on the edge of an enormous diving board with his arms outstretched. Sean looked down at Katie and gave her a strange, almost confused look.

"Thank you!" he called out. Then he dived gracefully into the pool with barely a splash.

"Outstanding dive!" called out Georgio. Squid, who was sitting on his dad's shoulders, clapped.

The Space Brigade, Princess Petronella, and the Gorgioskios were all enjoying a swim in the pool on the Royal Spaceship. The princess had offered to give the Earthlings a lift back to Earth, and although Tyler was sorry not to have the chance to use the Mini Easy-Ride Spaceship again, they hadn't been able to resist the chance to use all the Spaceship's incredible facilities as it flew through space.

There were huge windows all along the side of the swimming pool and Nicola could see the planets of Volcomania and Whimsy silently floating in space, joined by the cylinder that was the Underground Sea. From this height,

Volcomania's erupting volcanoes were like tiny matchstick flames.

"It looks so peaceful from up here," commented Mully. She, like the rest of them, was wearing a jewel-encrusted swimsuit from the Royal Spaceship wardrobe.

"Hopefully it will be peaceful from now on," said Nicola.

"Thanks to us!" said Princess Petronella, lazing back on a floating inflatable throne.

"You never told us how you and the aunts managed to infiltrate the enemy lines," said Nicola to Mully. "What was your secret weapon?"

"Age," said Mully.

"Pardon?" said Nicola.

"When you get to a certain age," said Mully, "you become invisible to young people. The aunts and I just walked on past those soldiers, saying things like, 'Excuse me, young fellow.' None of them took the slightest notice of us."

"And how did you sabotage their tanks?" asked Tyler. "Did you use some special technique from your army days?"

Mully smiled. "We threw away the keys. It's the simplest solutions that are the most effective."

"I always knew I'd married a genius," said Georgio.

When they had left the planet of Whimsy, Henry Sweet and Marty Mania were deep in discussion. Henry had already agreed that the Volcomanians could grow crops on Whimsy's lands, as long as there were still plenty of meadows left for lying around staring at the sky.

The United Aunts had stayed behind to help ensure the peace process continued peacefully. "I'll see you back at Grammy's birthday party," Great-Aunt Annie had told Nicola and Sean. Then she winked. "Maybe you won't call me Crazy Great-Aunt Annie in the future, eh?"

At the mention of Grammy's birthday party, Katie had remembered that they'd promised to bring something pink back for Nicola's little cousin Jessie. One of the Whimsians had given them the most beautiful handmade doll wearing an exquisite pink ball gown. "I actually wouldn't mind keeping it myself," Katie had admitted to Nicola.

The Volcomanian soldiers hadn't gone home yet. An enormous dance party was underway with some of Whimsy's best rock bands playing. Volcomanian soldiers had already proposed marriage to Poppy the waitress/actress and Rosie the beautiful preschool teacher.

Mrs. Mania had been untied from her chair, but was refusing to budge. "All this *niceness* is making me nauseous," she said, but Nicola noticed a spark of pride in her eyes as she watched her son transformed from toad to president. The United Aunts were arguing among themselves about the best punishment for Mrs. Mania, given that she had ordered the invasion of an innocent planet and the kidnapping of the United Aunts. Some of them (like Nicola's great-aunt Annie) were arguing she should be exiled on the planet of Arth for her actions. Other, cuddlier-looking aunts were saying, "Oh, let's just insist she *apologizes*."

The prison camp guards had also been released from their chairs in the food hall and were following Marty's orders to pull down the camp. It had been especially satisfying to see the guard who reminded Nicola and Sean of the school bully sweating and swearing as he pulled down the barbed wire fence he'd ordered the prisoners to polish.

They hadn't needed their scuba diving suits again. Marty Mania had arranged for them to travel back through the Underground Sea in comfortable Volcomanian submarines.

When they got back to Volcomania, Shimlara had proudly showed off her bus driving skills to her parents and brother, and driven them back to the stone hut where the Globagaskarian secret agent JJ-11 had been waiting for them.

"I hear you not only achieved your mission but you actually helped the Whimsians win the war!" said JJ-11. "I eat my words. When I first met you at the bottom of that pile of volcanic ash, I thought you were giggling fools, but you really did live up to the Space Brigade's reputation!"

As Nicola dived beneath the water of the Royal Spaceship pool, her hand went to her neck where her limited edition gold button had once been, and she thought about how close the Space Brigade had been to *losing* their reputation.

She swam to the surface.

"Hey!" she called out to the others. "Did anyone use their gold buttons to fix a mistake?"

The rest of the Space Brigade swam over to her.

"I've still got mine." Tyler held up the button still hanging around his neck.

"I used mine," admitted Katie. "I made a *terrible* mistake that would have lost us the battle. I was too soft on my music platoon. I didn't make them practice enough. It was so embarrassing. The drums didn't sound anything like hooves! The Volcomanians burst out laughing. They were on to us right away. I'm so relieved I got a second chance to fix that mistake!"

Nicola remembered how she'd been surprised at Katie's sternness with her platoon.

"I used my button, too," said Greta. "My mistake was the opposite. I was too mean to my platoon. Nicola told me I should encourage them and that sort of . . . irritated me. So I did the opposite. Next thing, all the writers and poets had walked off in a huff and convinced all the other Whimsians to pull out of the battle. It was terrible!" She paused. "Although I still think they were big crybabies and we shouldn't have had to coddle them like that."

"Aha!" Nicola pointed at Greta. "I knew it was strange when you were so nice to me!"

Greta narrowed her eyes at Nicola. "Wait a minute. What about that time you hugged me outside the food hall. That was so weird! I bet you'd come back in time to fix a mistake, right?"

Nicola admitted she was right and told them what had happened.

"Wow," said Shimlara. "And all along I thought my mistake must have been the worst. You made some doozies! All I did was drive the school bus off the crater of a volcano."

"You *didn't*!" said Tyler. "When?"

"It was when we came back to Volcomania after we'd won the battle," said Shimlara. "I was in such a good mood, showing off, driving too fast, and next thing you know, we were sailing through the air into a live volcano. You were all screaming, *'Unbutton your mistake!'* So I did, just before we hit the lava."

"I'm glad I have no memory of that," said Katie. "That must have been terrifying."

Nicola looked at Sean and saw that his button was missing from around his neck, too.

"Ha! You messed up, too! Confess!"

Sean looked embarrassed.

"I used it about thirty seconds ago," he said.

"What? You made a mistake while we were swimming in the pool?" said Greta.

"It was when I was on the diving board," admitted Sean. "Katie said, 'Be careful,' so I did an extra big bounce. The diving board is made for Globagaskarians and it's extra bouncy. I hit the spaceship roof headfirst and when I landed I hit my chin against the side of the pool. I think I broke my arm and my mouth was full of broken teeth and blood. It was the worst pain I'd ever experienced. So, yeah, I was pretty happy to unbutton that mistake."

"You idiot," said Greta.

"That's what you said the first time," said Sean.

"So Tyler is the only one who hasn't made a mistake," said Nicola.

"I guess I'm just perfect," said Tyler.

"I wish we had an endless supply of those gold buttons," sighed Katie.

"Don't worry," said Tyler. "If you make another mistake, you can use mine."

"What are you all talking about so seriously?" Princess Petronella had paddled her inflatable throne over to join them.

"Mistakes," said Shimlara.

"I don't know anything about mistakes," said the princess. "What's it like to make one?"

"Didn't you make a mistake ordering Earth to be destroyed?" said Nicola.

"Nope," said the princess. "Because otherwise I would never have collected so many dear friends!"

"Oh, that's sweet," said Katie.

"Except we're not *stamps*," said Greta.

A message came over the spaceship loudspeaker. "Attention, all passengers. Our estimated time of arrival on Earth is approximately twenty minutes."

"I wonder how much time will have passed on Earth," said Nicola as they all climbed out of the pool and dried themselves. "Hopefully only a few minutes, so no one will have missed us."

It was very strange to think of returning to ordinary life after they'd parachuted over volcanoes, scuba dived through the Underground Sea, white water rafted, and then helped a planet win a war.

"I assume you flew on Time-Squeeze speed, so you had time up your sleeve," said Georgio.

"We always do," said Nicola.

"That's good," said Georgio. "Because if you hadn't, I calculate that at least ten years would have passed in Earth time. Imagine that! Your parents would have spent the last ten years worrying about you. All your friends would be ten years older. You would—oh my goodness, are you *choking*, Tyler?"

Everyone turned to look at Tyler. His face had gone white.

"I *forgot*," he wheezed.

"Forgot what?" said Nicola.

"I made a terrible mistake! I forgot to put the spaceship on Time-Squeeze speed! Ten years will have passed! I— what? Why are you all pointing at me?"

Suddenly he understood. He grinned at them, and holding the gold button between his fingertips, he began to murmur, "Let that moment retake . . ."

Nicola blinked. She had a slightly odd feeling. She wasn't sure why. Georgio was in the middle of saying to Tyler, "I assume you flew on Time-Squeeze speed, so you had time up your sleeve."

For some reason Tyler's face was bright pink and his glasses were fogged up. He spoke slowly, as if he was dazed. "I fixed my mistake."

"What mistake?" asked Nicola. She had no idea what Tyler was talking about.

Tyler took his glasses off and polished them with his sleeve. "That was the most amazing thing! I went right back to when we first left Earth in the spaceship and this time I made sure we went on Time-Squeeze speed! It was incredible!"

Ah. So Tyler had made a mistake and now he'd fixed it. It was so strange that Nicola had no memory of it happening. Now everyone had used their limited edition gold buttons, so there would be no more second chances.

We'll just have to live with our mistakes from now on, thought Nicola.

Everyone was concentrating on Tyler, so she was the only one to catch the first glimpse of Earth's familiar curve through the spaceship window. Seeing Earth from outer space was like seeing her own life from very far away. She thought about all the tiny things that could upset her on an ordinary day: missing the bus, homework, an argument with Sean. She vowed that at least once a day she would stop and remember that somewhere in the galaxy, planets were at war, fighting for the freedom she took for granted: the freedom to be annoyed by little things, because you didn't have to be terrified by much bigger things. Of course, it wouldn't stop her from being annoyed by Sean or wishing she didn't have homework, but it might help her put things in perspective.

As the Royal Spaceship plummeted back into Earth's outer atmosphere, Nicola's heart lifted. She thought about all the ordinary places and things and sights and sounds that lay waiting for her: her mom's frown as she sorted mismatched socks from the wash and yelled out answers to the quiz show on TV, her dad dancing around the kitchen as he burned the lamb chops, the taste of cheese on toast, the feel of her own pillow at the end of a long day, the shrill cries of cicadas as Earth's only sun slipped down toward the horizon outside her bedroom window.

Earth wasn't a perfect planet, but it was hers.

Home, she thought. *It's so good to be home.*

THE END

LIANE MORIARTY

had her first story published when she was ten years old. Her mother still thinks it's the best thing she's ever written. Since then she's written seven novels for adults set in the real world and three books for children set in outer space. Some of her books have been number-one best sellers and one has even been made into a TV series.

When she is not writing, she's either eating chocolate, reading in the bathtub, or standing on the side of the soccer field yelling out helpful advice to her children, even though she actually has no idea how to play.